Frogs and Snails and Puppy Dog's Tales

Frogs and Snails and Puppy Dog's Tales

Short Stories from Ireland
A Children's Book for Adults

By

Frank Murney

Order this book online at www.trafford.com
or email orders@trafford.com

Most Trafford titles are also available at major online book retailers.

Printed in the United States of America.

ISBN: 978-1-4269-6136-6 (sc)
ISBN: 978-1-4269-6353-7 (hc)
ISBN: 978-1-4269-6352-0 (e)

Library of Congress Control Number: 2011905569

Trafford rev. 06/09/2011

www.trafford.com

North America & International
toll-free: 1 888 232 4444 (USA & Canada)
phone: 250 383 6864 ✦ fax: 812 355 4082

'Book 1 of the Newry Tales Series'

Ten-year-old Red Morgan and Po Hillen are the best of friends growing up in Newry, Northern Ireland, in the late 1950s. It's an adventurous time for these boys who always seem to be at the centre of a little mischief.

At school, they are part of a class known as 3C. They are generally unruly, argumentative, manipulative, conniving, and devious, or, in the terms of the modern educationalist, a challenge. But these 3C students face their own challenges every day. They have to devise strategies well in advance of their classes to outwit their weary teachers, plan little ways to annoy, cajole, divert, and dodge. Outside school, their lives reflect the poverty and innocence of the times where they have some unbelievable and hilarious situations with often intriguing and hair-raising outcomes.

Through the eyes of Red and Po, Frogs and Snails and Puppy Dog's Tales takes a nostalgic journey through the streets, shops and cafés of Newry, a small picturesque town on the Irish border.

Dedicated to the memory of

Eileen and Vincie

Special Thanks to

Oliver Curran
Hazel Abdulla
Nancy Critchly
Sharon Oseas

*For their generosity of time,
encouragement
and talent.*

Characters

Due to the fact that the same characters appear in almost all the stories within, I hope it may be advantageous to describe them in advance rather than in each individual story.

Anto	Antonio Falsoni	Well built with black hair, swarthy complexion. He had a husky voice and a strong personality. He lived and worked in his uncle's café, Uncle Luigi's. Good sense of humour and was the 'Bookie' of the gang.
Blackie	Keith Havern	Tall, well built, and athletic. He had black short hair and always well dressed. A very good looking 11 year old.
Boots	Peter Markey	Small, thin, with dark hair that always seemed to stick up at the crown of his head. 11 years old and a good footballer. He loved wearing boots, hence the nickname.
Dunno	Peter McManus	Small, brown haired 11 year old, best mate of Jumpy Jones. His answer to most questions was, 'Dunno'.
Ginger	Thomas McVerry	Small 11 year old, ginger haired lad with a round 'cheeky' face. A good footballer and runner. He was an excellent climber.
Jammy	Tommy McAteer	A dark haired, good looking 11 year old. He was an excellent footballer and a good all round athlete. He was fond of chatting up the girls. Very lucky or 'Jammy'

Jumpy	Francis Jones	A tall skinny blond 11 year old. Rivalled his mate Dunno in the brains department, but with a good sense of fun. Could never stand still and was always being asked to stop jumping around.
Kitter	Tommy Murray	Freckle faced, ginger haired lad with a very loud infectious laugh, always telling jokes. Left handed, hence the nickname.
Lanky	John Larkin	Tall and thin with large blue eyes and blond hair. Ungainly in posture but a good runner.
Pajoe	Patrick Joseph McArdle:	Red Morgan's uncle, small, grey haired stout man with a round ruddy face. Always in a jolly mood. Carpenter by trade.
Po	Oliver Hillen	Small with black curly hair, hooked nose and a swarthy complexion. He was the 'ideas' man of the gang, a few months older than Red. It was never discovered where the nickname 'Po' came from but Red suspected it had something to do with his 'Potty' when he was a baby.
Red	John Joseph Morgan	A tall, well built, athletic 11 year old with a mass of red hair that was unkempt during the week, but well Brylcreemed for the dances at the weekends.
Roberto	Roberto Falsoni	Small, balding, swarthy, stubby man who worked in the café for Uncle Luigi, mostly with Ice Cream sales. In his early 40s. Uncle Luigi's son.

Shifty	Jimmy McShane	Small, brown haired, freckle faced 11 year old who enjoyed gambling. Always on the look out for ways to make money.
The Bishop	Peter Keenan	Tall, rather studious looking with glasses. Dark blond hair, always neat, took pride in his dress. Everyone thought he looked like a clergyman. Good Chess player.
Topcoat	James Anderson	The odd one out in the gang. A small, thin, wizen faced man with a lisp and a mop of ginger hair. He was about 40 years old. He lived in a little cottage on his own outside Camlough village. He would have been considered eccentric.

Places

Due to the fact that many of the same places appear in almost all the stories within, I hope it may be advantageous to describe them in advance rather than in each individual story.

Uncle Luigi's Cafe	Situated on Newry's main street, Luigi's was a local meeting place for all the gang. One of Red and Po's best friends, Anto Falsoni, worked there part-time for his uncle and café owner, Luigi Falsoni. The café had an ice cream counter on the left when entering. Next on the left was the Jukebox. On the right there were five 'Snugs' with high backed seats and a fixed table in the centre. On the left of the café there was a collection of gingham covered tables and chairs. At the far end was the 'Chip Counter'. There could be found Luigi's pride and joy, the great glistening chrome chipper. It had a painted Italian beach scene on its upper part, and it was said to produce the best 'Fish and Chips' in Ireland.
The Bucket	An old, flat roofed hall found halfway along Castle Street at the corner of the hill of Hyde Market, directly facing the famous McCann's Bakery. The hall itself was said to have been originally the Abbot's house. There was a tunnel running from the building under Castle Street to the old Abbey grounds which was said to be the way the Abbot went every morning to say mass, as he was not allowed to be seen by the public. The dance floor was upstairs and was reached by a steep climb of thirty steps at the Hyde Market End. A large cross was positioned in front of the hall looking down towards the town.
The Florentine	Positioned at the centre of Hill Street, a well known local, Italian owned cafe, famous for its frothy coffee and good quality food.

The Savoy Cinema	Located at the corner of Monaghan Street at the canal bridge. The most modern of the local cinemas it was well known for its balcony, or as it was known locally, 'The Gods'.
The Imperial Cinema	Located on The Mall. The smallest of the local cinemas and without doubt, the most ancient. When the time came to start the movie, the ticket collector would walk to the stage and open the heavy velvet curtains to expose the screen to allow the movie to begin.
The Frontier Cinema	Located on John Mitchell Place, a continuation of the main street, Hill Street. This was a favourite for a number of reasons. Firstly, it was only a few hundred yards from Castle Street. Secondly, Red and Po had found a way to gain entrance without having to pay. Thirdly, they had a morning session every Saturday in which there was a Talent Competition on stage for the local kids before the movie began. They also were well up to date on all the Serials, like The Lone Ranger, Superman, Batman and Robin, and such like.
The Nun's Graveyard	A large park type hillside behind the St. Clare's Convent. It was surrounded by an eight foot wall. The area inside the wall was a well kept grassy area with plants and many large oak trees and weeping willows. Looked upon as a 'spooky' place at night.
The Parochial Hall	Located at Downshire Road, near the Town Hall, this was a place which booked the top Showbands in Ireland. Every weekend it would be packed to hear music from The Royal, The Freshmen, The Miami, The College Boys, The Clipper Charlton and many more. No alcohol was served, just coffee, tea, soft drinks and milkshakes.
The Baths	Warrenpoint Swimming Pool. Filled daily with sea water and unheated. There were two diving boards, a low one and a high one.

Newry Town Centre
1950

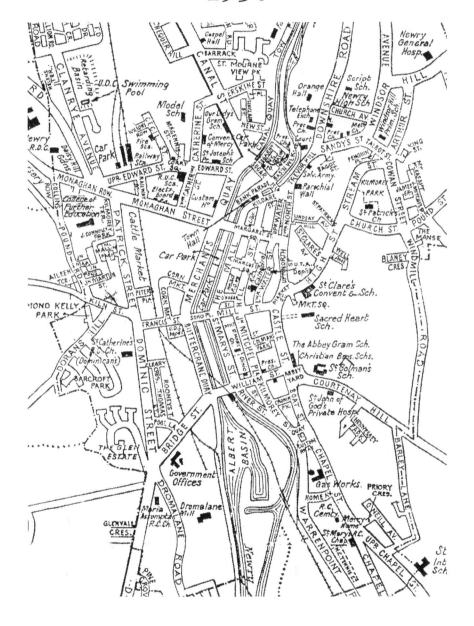

Contents

The Airfield

1957

Red and Po finally reached their destination two miles south of Dundalk. They turned their bikes onto a lane on the left of the road and stopped.

"Is this it?" asked Po.

"Yeah, I think so…see the wind sock?" said Red, as he pointed to an orange hollow cloth tube fluttering in the wind at the top of a pole some one hundred and fifty yards away.

"What's a wind sock anyway?"

"Shows the pilots which way the wind is blowin' when they are takin' off and landin'…come on," said Red, pushing off on his bike.

They had arrived at Dundalk Airfield. This field was used by local light aircraft owners in the County Louth area. There was a small hanger which would have held three, possibly four planes, and a small wooden office which doubled as Air Traffic Control. It was Sunday and Red had decided he wanted to go to the airfield to watch the planes coming and going. They followed the lane until they reached a small car park. The place was deserted, no cars, no people, and just one small orange and white Cessna 150 parked outside the hanger.

"Where's all the planes?" asked Po looking around.

"How do I know?"

"Well, are we stayin' here or what?"

"Don't know, we'll wait for a wee while to see if any come in, huh?"

"Suppose so."

They sat down on the grass, lit up two Woodbines and waited. After about an hour of inactivity at the airfield a mutual decision was made to go home.

"Hang on a minute, I need a leak," said Po, heading over to a tree beside the wire fence that separated the lane from the car park and the airfield. Red got on his bike and was riding around in circles when he heard a loud scream. He skidded to a stop and looked in Po's direction. Po was rolling on the grass beside the ditch moaning and holding his groin.

Red jumped off his bike and raced to his side.

"What happened?"

Po just groaned.

"Po, what happened?" said Red, his voice raised in concern that Po had seriously hurt himself. Po still didn't answer, he just groaned. Red knelt down beside him.

"Come on Po for Christ's sake, what happened ta ya?"

"Ahaaa, I don't know, pain in my bollocks, it's very bad," moaned Po starting to kneel.

"Did ya catch it on somethin'?"

"No."

"Are ya sure?"

"Frig off."

"Well, what the hell did ya do?"

"How the frig do I know, I just got this terrible pain in my thing. It went all through my body."

Po was now standing up.

"Is it gone?"

"Yeah, suppose it is. Christ that was sore."

"We'll call into the hospital just in case."

"I'm not goin' ta any friggin' hospital."

"Are ya ok ta ride your bike?"

"Yeah, Jasus, never felt a pain like that before I can tell ya."
"Ya need ta get that checked out, it might be serious ya know."

The boys got on their bikes and headed back up the airfield lane. When they reached the end, they stopped to wait for a break in the traffic to get across the main road. Po went on ahead of Red who was fixing the bag on the back of his bike. When Red looked up he noticed a red and white sign on the fence. It was partly covered by the hedge. He had to read it at least three times to be sure his eyes were not playing tricks on him. Po looked back but couldn't see Red. He stopped, turned and went back toward the airfield lane. When he got there he found Red sitting in the ditch head in hands, laughing.
"What?"
"Jasus Christ...I have met some ejits in my life, but you take the biscuit."
"What, will ya tell me ya bastard?"
"Can ya not read, moron?"
"Read what?"
Red launched into another burst of laughter and just pointed at the sign. Po read the sign, looked at Red, back at the sign, back at Red.
"You mean that I..." Po pointed at the sign.
"Yeah, ya moron, did no one ever tell ya never to piss on an Electric Fence?"

End

The School Play

1958

It was just past eleven that Thursday night in 1958, when the two shadowy figures stopped at a secluded part of the fence surrounding St. Joseph's Intermediate School in Newry. Red gave Po a final push to help him over and watched as he disappeared into the darkness on the other side. The silence of the night was shattered by a loud crash followed by soft moaning.

"Po?" Red whispered through the fence, "are ya ok?"

The stream of obscenities coming from the other side assured Red that, if Po was not all right, at least his mouth was in perfect working order. He clambered over the fence with a little more ease than Po managed; perhaps this was, in part, due to the fact that Red was at least twelve inches taller and by far the more agile. He found Po nursing his leg.

"What happened ta ya?"

"Nothin', nothin' a'tall…other than the fact that I nearly broke ma friggin' neck… that's all!" snarled Po.

"Then why are ya rubbin' your leg?"

"You're a real funny bastard; do ya know that, Morgan?"

Red just grunted and moved off into the darkness.

"Come on," he whispered over his shoulder.

"Come on, come on," mimicked Po. "I could be badly injured ya know."

Sympathy was in short supply…there was no response.

Red and Po made their way along the bushes to the school building keeping themselves hidden from the houses on the main road. A few moments later Red stopped under a small window.

"Right, here we are."

"Ya know somethin', ya haven't told me yet why the hell we're here," said Po looking directly into Red's face.

"I'll tell ya later."

"Ya'll tell me now, Morgan."

Red knew Po could dig his heels in when he wanted to, so the best thing to do was give him a little information…just enough to keep him happy.

"Look, it's like this, ya know that creep Fallon, the drama teacher? Well, as ya know, he's not too fond of me. He's insistin' that I take part in the School Play," explained Red.

"So?"

"So, all the costumes for the play arrived this afternoon. Now, if for some reason the costume that I'm supposed ta be wearin' at tomorrow's dress rehearsal is missin'…" Red held out his hands inviting Po to finish the sentence.

"Now I have ya, no costume, no Red in play," finished Po.

"Po, sometimes I just can't believe how friggin' smart ya are."

"Piss off."

"Right, this is the window," said Red looking up at the aperture some five feet above the ground. I left it open this afternoon. Lemme give ya a lift," said Red without looking at Po.

"Hold on a friggin' minute, why can't ya go in first?"

"Po, get a grip! Look at the size a me. There's no way I could get though that window," said Red with all the sincerity he could muster.

"So muggins here has ta go in…right?"

"Po, wait till I tell ya. You're the best friend…"

"Red?"

"Yeah?" answered Red sweetly.

"Did I ever in my life tell ya ta frig off?"

"Well, once or twice."

"Then, add this ta your list...frig off!"

"Ah come on Po, ya wouldn't let a mate down in a time of need, would ya?" pleaded Red.

"You're right, I wouldn't let a mate down in a time of need," said Po as he turned to go. Red reached out and grabbed him by the shoulder, spinning him around.

"Do I have ta remind ya of the time that, if it wasn't for me, your da would have..."

"Now hold on Red. Ya said ya would never throw that up," muttered Po.

"I lied."

"Look, if I go in here, will ya give me your word of honour...wait a minute, ya don't have any honour. If I go in here will ya promise on your mom's life that we're quits?"

"Ya got it."

"I'd be better off with a mangy dog for a best friend," grumbled Po.

"Go on, get in will ya!"

"You're a bastard Morgan."

"Ach Po, I love ya too…give us a kiss."

"Away and frig off ya fruit."

"Will ya hurry up for Christ's sake?"

"All right, all right…Hi, what do I do when I'm inside?" asked Po.

"Go down the corridor and into the gym. Then go to the emergency doors at the other end and open them. I'll be waitin' outside."

Red leaned his back against the wall and cupped his hands giving Po a step up. He had both legs through the open window and was about to drop inside when he stopped as if he had thought of something. He looked at Red standing in the darkness.

"Bastard face!"

"Shithead!" answered Red.

Po smiled and disappeared through the window.

Red hurried around the corner of the building and along to the emergency doors at the far end of the gym. Once there he waited and listened, all was quiet. He knew it would take Po a few minutes to get to the doors.

Both Red and Po were in the same class at school. They were the same age, well, almost. Red was twelve and four months, Po was twelve and six months. Po never let Red forget this small detail. 'I'm older than you Morgan therefore I'm more experienced in life.' Red would usually smile and let the comment go unanswered. He knew Po would not be satisfied until he thought he had got one over on him.

'Well? Are ya afraid of the truth Morgan?' Po would say.

'See, ya have nothin' ta say have ya Morgan?' This usually made Po's day. To get one over on Red was a big thing to him. Physically, Red was the larger of the two. In fact he was the tallest in his year at school, but not skinny in his six foot frame. A natural athlete, he was involved in many sports. This built up his legs and upper body to such an extent that he appeared older than his years. He had a mass of auburn hair which was always untidy during the week, but well groomed on the weekends when he and Po went to the dances. Po on the other hand was small and slightly built, standing about five foot. He had a swarthy complexion and black curly hair. Red teased him about this, 'I think you look like one of those gypsies he would say.' Po would never let Red get away with anything if he could help it. 'So what, I'd rather look like a gypsy than a toffee apple.' This kind of remark usually ended up in a wrestling match between the two.

Red's thoughts were interrupted by Po's voice from inside the doors.

"Red...you there?"

"No, I'm away home ten minutes ago. Open the friggin' door ya ejit."

A moment later the door opened and a breathless Po stood there holding his chest.

"Bastards, dirty rotten bastards," panted Po.

"What happened?"

"Them bastards...them lazy bastards...they left the ropes and stuff out in the gym," panted Po struggling to get his breath.

"So what?"

"So what?" panted Po.

"I'll tell ya so what...I ran into the friggin' ropes didn't I...didn't know what they were...scared the shit outta me...bastards!" Po paused for breath. "Then I fell over a stupid friggin' mat into that friggin' horse thing."

Red had tears running down his face. He was doubled over, arms wrapped around his waist as if to keep something from falling out. He was shaking from head to toe.

"Oh aye, go on, have a good laugh, ya shithead."

There was no answer from Red. He was trying his best to get control of himself but was finding the task difficult. Po couldn't see the funny side of things. He stared at Red as if he'd gone funny in the head.

"Are ya the full shillin', are ya? There's nothin' friggin' funny about it."

It took another few minutes before Red had settled himself enough to speak to Po.

"Right…ok…let's get this thing organised," said Red, trying hard to sound convincing.

"Look Red…a joke's a joke, but I could've had a heart attack back there ya know."

"Po, do me one small favour…shut up," Red pleaded.

Po continued mumbling obscenities as he followed Red into the darkness of the gym, half of his words aimed at Red and the other half at the last class to use the gym that day. Eventually they arrived at the storeroom in the assembly hall. Red opened the door and entered. When they were inside, Red fumbled around for the light switch until he found it. There were no windows in the room and Red knew light would not be seen from outside. It took a few moments for their eyes to get adjusted.

"Right, start looking," said Red pointing at about a dozen cardboard boxes stacked on one side of the small room. "…and don't leave a mess. I don't want anyone ta know we've been here."

"What do I look for?"

"All the costumes have name tags on them, look for the one with my name on it stupid."

"Oh! I'm awful sorry for breathin'. "

"Go, go and start lookin' will ya or we'll be here all night."

It took Red almost five minutes to find what he was looking for.

"Right, I got the bastard…let's go…and leave everythin' back nice and neat."

He stuffed the costume under his jacket.

Some fifteen minutes later, after retracing their steps, they were back on the main road walking towards town.

"Gis a smoke," said Po.

They stopped and Red produced a packet of Woodbine. After they had both lit up, Po inhaled deeply and looked at Red.

"Hi, ya never told me, what were ya in the stupid play anyway?"

Red looked away.

"Nothin', it doesn't matter now."

Po noticed a piece of the costume hanging down from under Red's jacket. Like a flash he had hold of it and pulled it out. Dancing with delight Po held the costume up in the air avoiding Red's attempts to grab it back. Po's eyes were as wide as saucers. He was roaring at the top of his voice.

"I don't believe it! I don't friggin' believe it! No wonder ya were in such a flap to get this costume, ya bastard."

"Po, I swear, ya mention this ta anybody, and I mean, anybody, and you're dead."

Po didn't hear. He was too busy dancing around the road with Red's costume held up in front of him.

"I don't believe it…a fairy…a friggin', whorin' fairy," roared Po.

Red chased Po all the way home but never caught him. At last Po had something on Red. All his birthdays had come at once that day!

End

The Nun's Graveyard

1958

It was closing time that Friday night when Red Morgan arrived at Luigi's Café. Uncle Luigi, as everyone called him, was just about to lock the door when he saw Red.

"Come in…come in," he greeted Red with his usual broad, toothless grin.

"You lock door for Luigi, huh?" as he handed Red the keys. No answer was required. Uncle Luigi turned and waddled back up to the counter where his last six customers were waiting for their take-away fish and chips. He was a small, stout, bald man in his sixties who Red imagined going to bed in his apron. In fact, he couldn't remember ever seeing him 'apronless!' Red just nodded. He knew that Uncle Luigi really wanted him to stand at the door, keep it locked, and let the customers out when they had been served. This meant standing at the door for at least another fifteen minutes.

When all the customers were gone, Red helped with the cleaning up and floor washing. Also lending a hand that night were Blackie Havern, Naffy McKay and Topcoat Anderson. When the place was shining like a new pin they sat down in the front snug to the fish suppers that Uncle Luigi laid on for the lads who helped clean up. Red was the last to be seated having just finished putting the bins out back. As he approached the snug there was, as usual, a finger pointing debate in progress.

"That's rubbish!" Topcoat was saying angrily. His face was red with the effort of making his point. Topcoat was rather the odd man out at the table. He was in his forties, with a small thin body always covered from head to toe with an army Great Overcoat. He had a thin wizened face and a mop of unkempt, thinning, ginger hair. Topcoat, named for obvious reasons, lived in a little cottage outside the village of Camlough. Every day he would walk the four miles to Newry and home again.

"I walk home every night in the pitch dark past the graveyard at Mullan's Hill. If there were any ghosts don't ya think I mighta seen one over these past twenty years?" argued Topcoat slamming his fist on the table.
"Well, I can only tell ya what I've heard from a lot of people, and not the sort of people ta make up stories," Anto came back with equal force.

Antonio, or Anto as he was known, was Uncle Luigi's nephew. He was a good friend of Red's and a year older. Red caught Anto's eye as he squeezed into the snug. An almost imperceptible wink alerted him that Anto was 'at it' with Topcoat. Red knew he was up to something… but what? Whatever it was, he knew that Anto would expect him to be his back up. Red looked at Topcoat and thought to himself, 'What are ya walkin' into now ya bloody ejit?'
Anto looked at Red.
"Red, ya live up beside the Nuns. What's that graveyard like up there on the hill?"
"Well, let's put it this way, I wouldn't go into it late at night, I can tell ya that," replied Red hoping that this was the answer Anto wanted.
"There ya are, didn't I tell ya. Even Red wouldn't go near that place at night," said Anto sitting back in his seat with a satisfied look on his face.
"I'm surprised at ya Red," said Topcoat turning to look straight at Red.
"I thought ya would've had more sense."

"Well, I just think there are more things in heaven and earth and so on..." replied Red almost apologetically.

"Look, see you, Anderson, you're all talk. Sure ya might walk home through a hundred graveyards every night, but, this is the important thing, ya don't walk home through the Nun's Graveyard, do ya? " insisted Anto pushing home the point with his finger.

"Now hold on a minute here Anto, what are ya sayin'? Are ya sayin' I'd be afraid ta walk through the Nun's Graveyard?" Topcoat growled, getting even angrier. Almost in unison there followed a chorus of "Yeah."

"Right, that's it. No one tells me I'd be afraid ta walk anywhere. Ghosts? My arse. You lot are a bunch of wee girls. I'll walk through the Nun's Graveyard at any time of the night or day without a bother," boasted Topcoat sitting back and folding his arms with a smug look on his face.

"Aye, right, we believe ya. We all came up the friggin' canal on a bubble too," said Naffy McKay looking at Topcoat and grinning.

"Look, frig ya, frig all a ya. I'll prove it anytime ya say the word," puffed Topcoat, his face crimson. Red noticed the veins now protruding from his neck. He caught Anto's eye again and knew that Topcoat had just fallen into whatever trap had been set for him. 'The poor bastard,' mused Red.

"Well Red, whaddya think? How can we make Mr. Fearless here prove his point?" Anto sat back, looked up at the ceiling and continued... "We could let ya go up there now, but then if we did, that means we have ta go with ya ta prove ya did it, so that wouldn't work."

Topcoat jumped right in almost on cue. "I'll take somethin' with me and leave it anywhere ya like in the graveyard and ya can go back later ta prove I was there. Will that do, huh?"

"Well, whaddya think Red?" asked Anto.

"Sounds all right ta me," replied Red playing along.

"Right, I've got it!" Anto got up abruptly and left the snug.

"Back in a minute, don't disappear Topcoat."

"Don't ya friggin' worry yourself. I'm not gonna back out," said Topcoat sitting back and folding his arms again.

"Well if you girls will excuse me, I'm goin' ta meet my one," said Naffy getting up. "She finishes her shift in ten minutes."

"Give her one for me young Naffy," smiled Topcoat. His reply was just two fingers.

At that moment Anto arrived back and laid a hammer and a six inch nail on the table.

"Right, see that nail? I want ya ta hammer it into the big oak tree at the very top of the graveyard, ya know, at the top of the hill," smiled Anto. "Tomorrow Red and I will go back there ta see if ya did it. In fact I've even organised a lift up and back. I wanna be there ta see what excuse ya come up with ta back out."

"No chance Anto, I won't back out, don't ya worry yourself. Let's go right now."

Topcoat grabbed the hammer and nail. Anto held out both hands.

"Ok, so let's do it."

Topcoat was at the front door before Anto was even out of the snug.

"What are ya up ta ya bastard?" whispered Red to Anto.

"Tell ya up there."

Some ten minutes later the Ford Consul owned and driven by Anto's Uncle Roberto, parked half way up the steep hill of High Street opposite to what was locally known as 'The Rocks'. Anto had earlier informed Roberto of the plan, who thought the idea was insane, but agreed to go along despite his misgivings. Anto turned around to look at Topcoat in the back seat.

"Now, ya go across the rocks ta the bottom of the graveyard wall and..."

"I friggin' know where I'm goin'," snarled Topcoat getting out of the car.

"We'll wait here for ya, I think there's some smelling salts here somewhere…" said Anto, pretending to look in the glove compartment. "Ya might just need them. Are ya sure now that ya don't want ta back out…it's very dark up there…"

"Frig off," came the muted reply as Topcoat marched off into the darkness.

"Well?" asked Red looking at Anto. Even in the darkness of the car Red could see Anto had a grin on his face.

"Ok, right, we'll give him a five minute start, then, we'll follow. We'll get over the wall the way Topcoat went, and lay in the grass and wait on him comin' back. When he does, we'll reach out and…" Anto clamped his hands together, "grab the bastard's legs."

"Jasus, it'll freak him out altogether." Anto didn't hear Red's comment. He was in a fit of laughter at the thoughts of what might happen.

"You lot will end up givin' Topcoat a friggin' heart attack," commented Roberto.

Red and Anto waited the five minutes and quietly went off in the direction taken by Topcoat. A few minutes later they were over the wall of the Nun's Graveyard, lying face down in the long grass, one on each side of the path.

"He must be near the top by now," whispered Anto.

"I can't hear anythin', can you?" said Red.

"Naw."

A slight breeze rustled the trees in the darkness. Red looked around in the dim light.

'Jasus, this is a creepy place!' he thought.

He looked across at Anto who was lying beside a tree.

"Anto, this place would give ya the willies ya know?" whispered Red.

"Friggin' would, wouldn't it?"

"Do ya feel eyes in the dark lookin' at us Anto?"

"Morgan, don't ya start! I'm warnin' ya, ya bastard."

Just then they heard the sound of hammering. Anto giggled.

"He'll be on his way back in a few minutes, now shut up and get ready."

There was silence for a few moments, and then they heard a muffled shout, some more shouts, then, silence.

"Jasus. What the hell was that?"

Red didn't answer. One thing he knew for sure, Topcoat was in trouble.

"It sounds like someone's caught him, whaddya think?" asked Anto getting to his knees.

"Don't know," Red whispered.

"What'll we do?"

"We'd better go up the hill and see what happened."

They both waited a few more minutes and listened, but there were no more sounds.

Anto looked at Red and whispered, "Circle around huh?"

"Come on then," Red grunted as they both moved silently in a diagonal climb up the hill.

It took them about five minutes to slowly circle around to where they thought Topcoat should be. They were making sure they made as little noise as possible.

"Red, over here."

Anto's voice startled Red for a moment. He stopped and looked to his left. He could see Anto bending down. He moved quickly to his side. Topcoat was lying on the ground beside the big oak tree with the hammer still in his hand.

"What's wrong with him?" Red asked.

"I don't know, he's breathin' anyway. Have a quick look around just in case," Anto whispered.

Red only moved a few yards when he heard Anto's voice again.

"Ya stupid bastard."

Then he heard Anto lapse into laughter.

Red hurried back. He found Anto leaning against the tree bent in two with laughter.

"What?" pleaded Red. Anto couldn't answer. He just pointed at Topcoat. Red bent down to have a closer look and as he did he heard Anto get the words out...

"The stupid bastard thought somebody grabbed him..."

Red still hadn't figured out what was going on. Then he saw where Anto was pointing. Topcoat, in his haste, had hammered the nail though the tail of his own coat. When he tried to leave, it tugged him back. Thinking someone or something had grabbed him, he'd fainted!

Red fell back and erupted. He thought he was going to burst. Wrapping his arms around his sides on this occasion didn't help the pain at all. It took some time before they could get themselves together enough to revive Topcoat. But before they did, Red had an even more evil idea.

"Hold on a minute Anto. Before we get him up, suppose we pull the nail out of the tree and put it back again, get what I mean?" Anto looked at Red with a puzzled look on his face.

"We put the nail back in the tree, but not through his coat. We won't tell him what happened."

"Morgan you're a friggin' genius, brilliant, brilliant!"

Poor Topcoat still tells the story of how a dead nun reached up through the ground and grabbed him. At times like this, Red and Anto would swap glances, make their excuses, and quickly leave the company to find a place where they could lean on each other in fits of uncontrolled laughter.

End

A Day in the Life of Class 3C

1958

(1) The Religious Education Class

As the class settled down that morning, it was just the beginning of another day in the teachers uphill battle at St. Joseph's Boys School in Newry. Mr. Reed was first onto the battlefield that morning to face the nightmare known to all staff as 3C. It was his unenviable task, for an hour, to try and control, pit his wits against, and maybe, just maybe, get some knowledge to sink in. He knew deep in his soul it was a lost cause but he must at least try. Mr. Reed taught Religious Education. 3C was generally unruly, argumentative, manipulative, conniving and devious…in the terms of the modern educationalist, a challenge. But 3C students were not exactly who they appeared to be. They too faced a challenge every day. They had to devise strategies well in advance to outwit their weary teachers…plan little ways to annoy, cajole, divert and dodge. This made school far more interesting and challenging for them.

Mr. Thomas Reed stood at the head of the class reading from his Bible. He was at one time, it was rumoured, in a seminary, training to be a priest. A quiet, inoffensive man, almost too quiet one would think to be a teacher. Dressed usually in a dark suit, he looked more like a bank official.

"…and Christ ascended to his Father in Heaven," ended Mr. Reed. "Now 3C…"

"Sir…?" Dunno McManus put his hand up.

"Yes McManus?"

"Where is Paradise?"

"Paradise is where God dwells with His angels and saints."

"No."

"What do you mean, no, McManus?"

"No, Sir, that's not right, Sir."

"Of course it's right McManus, what on earth are you talking about?"

"Well Sir, Jesus doesn't agree with ya."

"McManus, you'd better have a very good explanation for that statement."

"Well, Sir, when Christ was on the cross He told your man beside him on the next cross that He'd be with him that day in Paradise."

"Right so far McManus, I'm impressed, go on."

"Well Sir, a couple of days later, in the garden Sir, where the tomb was, Christ was in fancy dress."

"He was what?"

"He was dressed up as a gardener, Sir," helped Red Morgan.

"Thank you Morgan. Please make yourself clear McManus."

"Well Sir, anyway He was dressed up as a gardener and your one, the Irish woman…"

"Irish woman…?"

"Mary McDillan Sir."

"Magdalene, McManus, Magdalene."

"That's her, Sir. She didn't know Him so she didn't."

"Class disguise," said Boots Markey.

"Quiet Markey."

"Anyway Sir, when your one…"

"Mary Magdalene."

"That's her Sir, finally recognized Him, she was gonna give Him a big hug and He wouldn't let her so He wouldn't."

"I think I'm still with you McManus."

"Well Sir, Christ told her not ta touch Him cause He hadn't been to see His Father in Heaven yet."

"So what? He had not yet ascended into Heaven McManus."

"Yes Sir I know, but He told the guy on the cross He'd be in Paradise with him on Friday, so here He was on Sunday telling your one…"

"Mary Magdalene."

"The very one Sir, that He hadn't been ta Heaven yet."

"Yes…I see…"

"So who's tellin' fibs Sir?" asked Red Morgan.

"Well you see…"

"Red, don't be stupid, J.C. can't tell lies, sure He's God!" spoke up Jumpy Jones.

"Can God tell lies, Sir?" asked Red Morgan.

"These are all very good questions class, which shows you are paying attention. I will deal with them next week. Now open your Bibles where we left off and read silently until I come back. As the classroom door closed Jumpy Jones was the first to speak.

"On the ball Dunno, we got him well today, what's the score Red?"

"Countin' last week, I make it 7 – 0."

"What's next week's one?" asked Boots.

"Next week's mine and it's a beauty," smiled Red.

Mr. Reed returned just before the bell to end the period.

"Right, 3C, make sure you read all the passages I gave you for the next class."

3C noisily exited the classroom and moved on to help Mr. Gray, the English teacher, get a little bit closer to his heart attack.

****

(2) *The English Class*

After what seemed an age, 3C settled down in Mr. Gray's class. He began the duel by handing out the graded homework assignments from the last class.

"Morgan!" shouted Mr. Gray.

"Yes Sir?"

"Get up here."

Red walked to the front of the class where Mr. Gray was pointing at a word in his homework.

"That is not a word you can use in a composition Morgan."

"It isn't Sir?"

"You know only too well it's not."

"I'm very sorry Sir, I didn't know."

"It's a swear word Morgan."

"Is it Sir?"

"Yes it is, don't use it again…sit down."

"Yes Sir."

Red returned to his seat giving 3C a wink on the way. He had just sat down when Jumpy Jones put his hand up.

"Sir?"

"Yes Jones."

"What word was it, Sir?"

"None of your business Jones."

"But it is Sir, like I might use it next week."

"That's right Sir," added Dunno McManus.

"I might use it too and then you'd be mad at me."

"Right 3C; now let's clear this up right now. Swear words are not allowed to be used in compositions."

"Sir?" Red had his hand up.

"Yes Morgan."

"It can't be a swear word, Sir."

"I said it is a swear word, Morgan."

"But Sir, it's in the Oxford Dictionary, Sir."

"That's not the point Morgan…"

"But Sir, if it's in the dictionary, Sir, it must be a proper word," added Bishop Keenan.

"Look, now get this straight…"

"That gives us an awful lot more work Sir, that's not fair," said Jumpy Jones.

"What are you talking about Jones?"

"Well Sir, from now on we'll have ta make a list of all the words in the dictionary we're not allowed ta use, Sir."

"Sir?"

"What Morgan?" Mr. Gray's patience was beginning to get strained.

"Are swear words not part of the English language, Sir?"

"Yes Morgan, some of them are but…"

"If they're part of the English language, Sir, why can't we use them?" popped in Shifty McShane.

"Most of you can't speak the English language in the first place McShane."

"I've never heard anythin' so stupid," said Bishop Keenan.

"What are you saying Keenan?"

"Them poor people who write the dictionary, they go ta all that trouble ta put words in it and even describe what they mean in all that detail, and then we're not allowed ta use them, Sir."

"Of course you can use them, Keenan, it's just…"

"But ya said we couldn't use them, Sir."

"You can't use them when…"

"But you're just after sayin' we could use them, Sir."

"Yes, but you can only use them…"

"Sir I wish ya would make up your mind, I'm all confused now," mumbled Red.

"Look, it's very simple…"

"Might be to you, Sir," said Jumpy Jones

"It is very simple to anyone with a brain. From now on, no swear words will be used, and that's that!"

Mr. Gray's face was reddening.

"Sir?"

"What now Morgan?" shouted Mr. Gray.

"Sir, I was just wonderin'…well…if we can't use the word in composition, can we use it when we're talkin'?"

"No you will not Morgan."

"But why is it in the dictionary a'tall, Sir, if we're not allowed ta use it?"

"Morgan," roared Mr. Gray.

"Yes Sir?"

"Get out of this class now you cheeky, impudent bastard."

"But Sir, I thought we weren't allowed ta use that word, Sir?"

The class erupted and Mr. Gray was a step nearer his heart attack.

****

(3) The Woodwork Class

Mr. Haig's Woodwork class was the last period before lunch. He seemed to be fighting a losing battle trying to get 3C to settle down. There was a constant din of chit-chat, laughter and general noise.

"For the last time...quiet!" bellowed the frustrated Mr. Haig who was coming perilously close to losing his patience. Instantly, there was complete silence. Mr. Haig almost flinched at its suddenness. However, he thought, 'Better make the best of it while it lasts.'

"Gather your projects from the cupboards and get your tools ready… quietly!" There was general industrious movement throughout 3C as they went about their tasks. This month the class was attempting to make small coffee tables.

Mr. John Haig was a tall balding man who managed to hold on to his sense of humour even with the non stop badgering of 3C. His dress remained the same it seemed throughout the year. A check shirt and tie, fawn trousers and brown brogue shoes.

There was a commotion at the far corner of the room. 'I knew it was too good to last,' thought Mr. Haig wistfully.

"McManus, what are you doing?"

"Shifty McShane's got my leg," Dunno McManus complained.

The class burst into laughter. Even Mr. Haig had to turn away trying to keep his face straight.

"Shifty, I didn't know ya were like that," commented Jammy McAteer.

"McAteer, go chew yourself," came back Shifty.

"My coffee table leg," said Dunno almost to himself.

"Ouch!" came a loud scream from the back of the class.

Jumpy Jones was running around holding the back of his neck. Ginger McVerry was standing, hands outstretched, with a very convincing expression of innocence on his face.

"McVerry, what did you do to Jones?" roared Mr. Haig, once again beginning to lose his patience.

"Sir, it's not my fault, Sir. He asked me ta take a blackhead outta his neck," pleaded Ginger. Mr. Haig took a deep breath as if to calm himself.

"McVerry, put those pliers down and get outside the class," Mr. Haig said slowly.

"That's the thanks ya get for tryin' ta help somebody," Ginger mumbled.

"Out!" Mr. Haig repeated, somewhat louder.

"Sir, can a tree feel pain?" asked Red Morgan with his chin resting on his hands.

"Morgan, what are you on about?" asked Mr. Haig.

"I heard that trees can feel pain, Sir," returned Red.

"Morgan, I don't know…and better yet…I don't care, just get on with it."

"I was only askin' a civil question, Sir, after all we're working on wood," said Red.

"Look, Morgan, if the wood starts to bleed let me know and I will take it to the First Aid room, ok?" Mr. Haig got a response of loud laughter from 3C.

"Red's right Sir, I heard that trees can feel pain," butted in Jumpy Jones.

"Look, I'm getting tired of this. I don't care one way or another. Just get on with your work, right?" Mr. Haig's face was getting flushed.

"Ah, that's terrible, Sir. I wouldn't fancy somebody like Shifty hacking at me with a chisel if I was wood," replied Red.

"Me neither," shouted Dunno. The class erupted again.

"Sir, Kitter Murray farted," shouted Jumpy Jones.

"Jones, that's not very nice," said Mr. Haig.

"Who are ya tellin', Sir? Ya wanna be down here," came the immediate reply.

Ten minutes later 3C had settled down again and was, in some way, getting on with their work.

Mr. Haig was seated at his desk reading a newspaper.

"Sir, why are we making coffee tables?" came the voice of Boots Markey.

"What?"

"Why are we making coffee tables, Sir?"

"Because that's what I want you to make."

"No, Sir, ya don't understand. Nobody I know drinks coffee, so why aren't we makin' tea tables?"

"Tea tables...? There's no such thing Markey."

"Why not? That's stupid. Why call a table a coffee table if all you're gonna' drink off it is tea?"

"Look, Markey, don't worry about what it's called, just get on with it."

"But a name is a very important thing, Sir," said Red Morgan.

"Morgan, just one word...don't."

"But Sir, if I was ta call a chisel a hammer, we'd never get a nail in."

"Morgan, look, I don't want a production made out of this. You seem to forget I know you people only too well. You might get away with fooling the other teachers, but you don't fool me."

"Ach, Mr. Haig, that's not fair. That was a good question about the coffee table so it was," spoke up Dunno. A general murmur of approval followed.

"No, you are not going to get me going this week…sorry…now get on with your work."

There was silence for about five minutes and then Red spoke up.

"Jumpy, what'll I do now?"

"Just bring your work over here ta I see it."

"What are you doing Morgan?"

"Who...me, Sir?"

"Yes, you Sir?"

"I was just askin' Jumpy what I should do next, Sir."

"Why?"

"Why what, Sir?"

"Why were you asking Jones what to do next?"

"Well, Sir, ya won't let us ask ya any questions, Sir."

"Don't be silly, Morgan, of course you can ask me questions providing...."

"Sir, why are these tables square and not round," asked Kitter.

"Because the plans..."

"Sir, I think my leg's broke," said Shifty.

"I told you not to force it in McShane."

"No Sir, not that leg, my leg. Boots Markey hit me with a mallet."

"What do ya call a Prison Warder in a car?" shouted the Bishop Keenan.

"What?" the whole class shouted.

"A Screwdriver."

"I have a good one," shouted Jammy McAteer. "What do ya get if ya cross a pig and a horse?"

"What?" the whole class shouted.

"A Ham-Mare." 3C was now in full flow.

"Right," roared Mr. Haig. "Get on with it. I'll be back shortly." 'I'm going for a smoke and a nervous breakdown,' he thought.

Mr. Haig left the class to their own devices, which he did every week. One of these weeks, he promised himself he would make it all the way through a complete class with 3C.

****

(4) The Second Religious Education Class

After lunch, 3C arrived outside Mr. Gain's classroom for their Geography lesson. The school secretary was there to redirect them back to Mr. Reed's classroom.

When they were seated, Jumpy Jones asked, "Sir, are you teachin' us geography today?"

"No, you are having an extra R.E. lesson because Mr. Gains is away this afternoon. Now, open your Bibles and finish reading the lesson about the Garden of Gethsemane."

A flurry of activity followed...then there was silence. 'Why me?' Mr. Reed thought, 'Having 3C once in a week is bad enough, but twice on the same day...'

Fifteen minutes later Mr. Reed looked up from the sports page of his newspaper.

"Now 3C, close your books and pay attention. So the Lord went three times to pray on His own after finding the apostles asleep. What can we learn from this...McManus?"

"The apostles were all drunk Sir?"

"No!...Jones?"

"Sir, I think they were just tired after all the walkin' about and stuff."

"Brilliant! So, we have learned today that Christ spoke to His Father in Heaven and asked Him what?...McVerry."

"It was somethin' about a chalice, Sir."

"And what did He say about this chalice…McVerry?"

"He didn't want it, Sir."

"Close enough McVerry, close enough, now..."

"Sir?"

"Yes Morgan?"

"Ya see that bit about Christ talkin' ta His Father, Sir, about the chalice and all that?"

"Yes Morgan," said Mr. Reed, a deep weariness beginning to creep into his voice.

"Well, when we were readin' it, the Bible that is…it said that the apostles were all sleepin' every time Christ came back ta them."

"Morgan, I think we can safely say we have established that fact."

"Sir, did none of the apostles even go and pray with Him?"

"No Morgan, He went off and prayed on His own. What is the point you are trying to make?"

"Well, Sir, it says that He asked His Father somethin' about a chalice."

"Yes Morgan, so what?"

"Who heard Him?"

"What?"

"Who heard Him talkin' ta His Father? Wasn't everybody asleep, Sir?"

"Well..."

"He had a tape recorder, Sir."

"Shut up McManus."

"I think some of the apostles were ear wiggin'."

"Jones, don't be stupid."

"But Sir, if none of the apostles heard Him and He didn't have a tape recorder how do we know what He said?"

"That's a very good question Morgan. I will deal with it in the next class. Now just get your Bibles open and read from where we left off… quietly! I don't want to hear a sound."

Mr. Reed left 3C to get on with their reading. As the door of the classroom closed, Red Morgan got hit on the back of the head with a rolled-up jotter.

"Nice one, Red, good job we had that one in reserve. We got him again. What's the score now?"

"8 - 0 at the moment."

****

(5) The P.E. Class

Mr. O'Brian, took a deep breath when he saw the first few 3C students burst into the Gym changing rooms. Dennis O'Brian was a small man, some might say good looking, with an athletic body and black curly hair.

"Hey Mr. O'Brian, are we playin' basketball today Sir?"

"No, football, Mr. O'Brian."

"No way, let's do the obstacle course, Mr. O'Brian."

"Will you all shut up! Get changed and get into the gym…now!"

Some ten minutes later 3C was in the gym, lined up and waiting for the fun to begin.

"Right, 3C, today we are going to concentrate on getting you lot fit."

The gym was filled with boos and hisses.

"Quiet!…Now, get out the climbing frames and the ropes," growled Mr. O'Brian assigning six students.

"The rest of you get the mats and the horses…move!"

Red Morgan was pulling out a climbing frame when he felt a tug on his shorts.

"Red, will we do the emergency stand by plan…whaddya think?"

"I think it's the perfect time, who's doin' it?"
"Jumpy Jones."
"Tell him ta make it good, right?"
"Right."

When all the equipment was in place, Mr. O'Brian instructed the class to form a line.
"Now, start here on the climbing bars and go all the way around the gym making sure to use every piece of apparatus."
Mr. O'Brian blew his whistle to begin the exercise. 3C started on their rounds of the gym with much moaning and groaning. A few moments later, Mr. O'Brian was attending to a sprained ankle. While he was examining the moaning student, there was a loud crash at the other end of the gym.
"Mr. O'Brian, come quick…Jumpy fell off the top of the ropes!"
Mr. O'Brian raced to a prostrate Jumpy Jones who was on the mat under the ropes. On a preliminary examination it was established that Jumpy was unconscious and needed medical treatment as soon as possible.
"Now, we can't move him in case there's something broken…McAteer, run to the office and ask Miss O'Keefe to ring for an ambulance…go!"
Jammy raced off at top speed.
"Now…Morgan, get a blanket out of the cupboard…the rest of you go and change…and stay quiet."

Later that day, Red Morgan and a few of the boys were standing chatting outside Uncle Luigi's Café. Jumpy Jones arrived wearing a broad grin.
"Hail the conquering hero," shouted Bishop Keenan.
A loud cheer went up from all as Jumpy was greeted with back patting and hair rubbing.
"Well, how much?"
"We went round everybody in the class and the best we could do was three shillin's' and sixpence."
"Have ta do I suppose, what happened ta you lot?"
"We got sent ta the playground for the rest of the class, great afternoon… and you?"

"Well, I woke up as planned, before the ambulance arrived. They made me go ta hospital anyway. I got orange drinks and chocolate biscuits and got sent home an hour later when ma dad arrived."

"Good day all round then…hi, Jumpy, loan us a shillin'."

"Ya have no chance, do ya realise the trauma I had ta suffer…the great pain and anguish ta get this?"

"Didn't know ya suffered that much, but I tell ya what…you're gonna…"

Red pulled Jumpy to the ground and the rest piled on.

And so ended another normal school day in the life of 3C. They had all gone home, had their dinners and went out to play. The teachers too went home, took their tranquillisers and checked their schedules for the next time they would encounter their living nightmare…3C.

Lay Low

1958

The street was filled with kids when Red closed the door behind him. Boots Markey came running past.

"Ya playin' Lay Low Red?"

"Yeah, is Po here?"

"He's in the shop."

"Right."

Everyone was gathering outside McCourt's old house in Castle Street waiting to get the game started. Two people in the crowd were selected to pick one person each and continue to do so until every last one was picked. Then there would be a coin toss to decide which side was away first. The game was a version of Tig. Usually the boys went in twos and if there were girls playing they did the same. The side that was away had a two block area in which to hide. This stretched from Mill Street to William Street and from Castle Street to Hill Street. The rules were very strictly adhered to. You were not allowed to cross the road on the boundary areas and you were not allowed to go into a house. It was also important that you told no one, your hiding place. Once someone was caught by the chasing side, he would then join them to seek out the rest of his team.

"Well," said Po coming up to Red, "what's the craic?"

"Nothin' new. Are we for the usual tonight?"

"For sure."

"Hi Red, I have a question for ya and Po. How come you two are never caught?" said Humpy Marron.

"There are a couple of answers to that Humpy. One, we have a great hidin' place and two, the guys searching for us are too stupid ta look in the right place."

"Is that so, well, I'll be lookin' for ya tonight."

"There ya go Po, another night without gettin' caught," said Red to a grinning Po.

"We'll see," sneered Humpy. "We have referees out tonight ya know?"

"Doesn't bother us, we stick ta the rules. We don't go in ta anyone's house, and we don't leave the area, so have yourself a good time runnin' around in circles lookin' for us," mocked Red.

Every so often, if there was a big crowd playing, the chasing team would select referees to stand around the area to make sure no one was breaking the rules. When the hiders had disappeared, the referees would rejoin the chasers to help with the search.

"Right!" shouted Kitter Murray getting everyone's attention.

"Hi Red, we'd better go a different way tonight with the referees out," whispered Po.

"Yeah, we'll go in from William Street."

"Ok, we're startin' the count to one hundred…go!"

Everyone of the hiders took off at speed in many directions, including Red and Po. They ran along Castle Street turning down William Street, stopping to ensure no one was watching. They climbed over a wall, across a number of gardens and over another wall until they reached an area known as Halans', a sort of communal, overgrown garden area. They reached the bottom and began climbing up a water pipe until they arrived at the top of a wall. From there they had to scale a second wall until they reached a flat roof. Once on the roof, they both sat down behind a chimney and, with cupped hands to hide the glow, lit up two Willie Woodbine cigarettes.

"What's the time now Red?" asked Po.

"Quarter to nine."

"Good timin', we have another fifteen minutes."

"Let's have a look," said Red as he crawled over to the three foot wall that surrounded the roof. Joined by Po, they slowly raised their heads to see what was going on below. They were using a good deal of unnecessary caution because, in the dark, there was very little chance of them been seen from the ground.

"Who's that?" whispered Red.

"Where?"

"Ya see the tree there, just a few feet behind it."

"That's that ejit Stoney Mavern with Pete Faloon. Ya can see that stupid cream jacket a mile away; there's more brains in a cabbage."

"I was just thinkin', I just love climbin' up drainpipes after you Po."

"Really? Why's that?"

"Ya have a lovely bum."

"Would ya ever piss off ya fruit."

"Hey, its nine o'clock, we need ta move."

Red led the way over one wall, down to another, onto a shed roof and down into an outside toilet. They opened the door and entered the darkness of the Frontier Cinema. They found two good seats and settled down to watch the movie.

Around an hour and a half later the boys turned from Hyde Market into Castle Street to see most of the gang were still there.

"Well, look who it isn't," said Red as they approached Humpy.

"Thought ya were supposed ta get us tonight?" asked Po.

"Don't worry, I'll find out where ya hide."

"Naw, not in this century Humpy," laughed Po.

Later that night the boys were talking to Jammy McAteer.

"Go on Red, give us a clue, where do ya hide?"

"A clue ya want?"

"Ah sure go on Red, give him a clue," said Po with a great smile across his face.

"Let's see now. We're not in the same place every week ya know. We travel all over the world."

"Ya need a Doctor, Morgan, ya know that?"

"Ya could be right."

Red looked at Po and they both gave each other a knowing smile. Red in fact wasn't lying about their whereabouts every week. Some weeks the movie was set in London, or Paris, Italy or Greece. In fact each week they were in a different part of the world and only they knew it.

End

Strange Knickers

1958

Not a single cloud appeared in the massive clear blue sky as the boys, and some girls, lay on the bank or splashed around in the County River on that glorious summer afternoon.

Red, Po and Anto were sitting together eating some sandwiches they had bribed or coerced their mothers into making for them. Bags and towels littered the area where the three were sitting. A pair of blue underpants caught Red's eye.

"Jasus, who owns the blue knickers?" he asked.

"They're Dunno's I think," answered Po. "Why?"

"Weird shade of blue, that's all," answered Red still staring at the underpants.

Sometime later Red was walking along the bank, when he heard his name being called.

"Hi Red, could ya give us a hand?"

Red turned to face a group of girls sitting close to the river's edge. He recognised the girl waving to him as Janet Daly, a pretty girl who lived on Mill Street just a few hundred yards from his house.

"Hi Janet, what's the problem?" asked Red as he approached the group.

"Stupid zipper's stuck on my bag," she complained.

"Let's see…" Red manoeuvred it a little and managed to get it open.

"There ya go, good as new," he smiled as he pulled open the bag.

Sitting neatly on top of Janet's clothes were a pair of knickers the exact colour of Dunno's underpants.

"Now Janet, don't take this the wrong way, but, are they a spare pair of knickers?"

Janet laughed loudly, "Yes they are, why, do ya want to borrow them? Didn't know ya were like that Red."

The idea had already lodged itself soundly in Red's mind. He explained to Janet his idea which made her clap her hands and giggle.

"Right now, do we all know what ta do?" asked Red as he finished explaining his plan to the gang.

"Yeah," said Po. I'll take him over ta get blackberries right?"

"We'll all get dressed quick and start headin' off," added Anto.

Just at that moment Dunno arrived after being in for a swim and began drying himself off.

"Well, are ya goin' ta go or not Po?" asked Red.

"Jasus, don't be gettin' your knickers in a twist, I'm goin'," came Po's smart answer.

Red had to look away and cough to stop himself laughing out loud.

"Dunno, will ya gis a hand ta get some blackberries?" asked Po getting up.

"Sure, no bother."

Po had already dressed and as soon as they had set off the rest of the gang began dressing quickly.

Po and Dunno were putting their blackberries in a plastic sandwich box when they heard Red's voice calling them.

"Come on Po and Dunno, we are headin' off home."

"Right Dunno, this'll do, come on, we'd better hurry."

"Jasus, I'm not even dressed yet," complained Dunno.

"Well, so, ya better hurry up then," said Po as he began running to catch up with the rest of the gang. When he did he grabbed Red.

"Did ya get his underpants…did ya?"

Red patted his pocket and smiled. Po looked over his shoulder to see how Dunno was doing and watched for a moment as he staggered around with one leg in his trousers trying to find the other one. The gang were back on the main road before a breathless Dunno, caught up with them.

They were about two miles from Newry and they weren't long into the journey before they noticed Dunno tugging at his underpants.

"What's the problem Dunno?" asked Red innocently.

"Friggin' things are too tight."

"Ya mean they got tight all of a sudden or were they tight before?"

"I don't remember them bein' tight before for sure," grimaced Dunno pulling at his trouser legs again.

"Will ya for Christ's sake leave them alone," complained Po. "People will think ya'r playing with yourself."

"Piss off Po will ya."

They all eventually arrived at Uncle Luigi's Café, ordered Cokes and sat in one of the snugs.

"De ya know what Dunno, ya haven't stopped pullin' at your trousers since ya left the County."

"It's these friggin' underpants; they're cuttin' the friggin' legs off me."

"Well, so loosen them then."

"Ya can't loosen underpants Red, don't be stupid."

"Under the label at the back, ya can loosen them. Isn't that right Anto?"

"Sure, I loosened mine yesterday; they got tight after they were washed."

"There ya go, stand up and turn around and I'll fix them for ya," said Red sincerely.

Dunno stood up and turned around loosening his belt and opening the top of his trousers.

Red pulled them down a little to the complaints of Dunno.

"Well Jasus Christ, ya dirty, kinky, twisted wee bastard."

"What?"

"Frig me, I don't believe it. All these years I've known ya Dunno. Played marbles and football with ya and I never knew."

"Knew what for frig sake?"

"That ya wore girl's knickers."

"Very funny, very funny."

"Let me see," said Po. "Jasus you're right Red, they're girl's knickers all right."

Dunno looked down at the garment in question and inspected them.

"These aren't mine," he pleaded.

"Dunno, ya don't have any sisters, so why are ya wearing girl's knickers… and would ya look, they even have wee flowers around the top…ya kinky wee bastard."

"But…I swear…they're not mine…they couldn't be…I don't know where they came from…honestly."

Dunno had now sat back down and had quickly done up his belt and trousers and had his now crimson face buried in his hands.

"Jasus…Jasus."

"Don't worry Dunno…we won't tell…many," laughed Anto.

"I don't understand…I don't understand…I swear ta God."

"Now Dunno, look…ya shouldn't be ashamed so ya shouldn't, it's all right being a fairy these days," said Po biting his lip.

Anto just could not keep it in any longer and just burst into almost hysterical laughter.

They let poor Dunno 'Knickers' McManus, as they now called him, stew, for almost three days before they told him how they tricked him.

"Yous are a bunch of bastards."

"We are…we are…" laughed Red.

"I'll get every single one of ya for this."

"Ya will…ya will…"

"Friggers."

To this day, Dunno was never allowed to forget. On occasion, he still gets called 'Blue Knickers McManus.'

End

God is Love

1958

Red was watching his mom's finger wagging under his nose. Mrs. Morgan was quite a small lady, perhaps just under five foot tall. Red stood a good twelve inches above her.

"That bedroom's a disgrace. I want it cleaned up properly and everything put away in its proper place. You'll not put your foot outside that front door until it's done, do ya hear me?"

"I'll do it now Mom, ok?"

"Yes ya will do it now, right now. I've asked ya a dozen times to clean up, but did ya pay any attention?"

Mrs. Morgan's hand caught Red on the ear before he had time to get out of the way. He often wondered how she could, for such a short woman, never ever miss the target.

"Did ya pay any attention?"

"No Mom."

"Don't 'no Mom' me," again with the hand catching him on the ear.

"Yes Mom."

"And don't 'yes Mom' me either," this time catching him with the other hand.

"I'm goin' ta clean it up now Mom."

"I'll inspect it when you're done too, go on then, what are ya waiting for?"

Red trudged up the stairs and went into his bedroom. Looking around his room he had to admit his mom was right, it was a mess. It looked as if a bomb had gone off. Thirty minutes later he was only just beginning to make some small inroads into the chaos.

He picked up a leather belt that had been lying concealed under his wardrobe. He had been looking for this belt for some time. Sitting down on the floor he inspected it and his mind was brought back some three years ago to when he was in Primary School. He was remembering the day Brother Feenan sent him to get his leather strap mended. It was the first Monday in October. The class were listening to the loud rasping voice of Brother Feenan in the last classroom on the top floor of the Abbey Primary School on Newry's Courtney Hill.

****

"I hope everyone has read and memorised the passages of Catechism I gave you yesterday…have you?"
"Yes Brother."
"Have you?"
"Yes Brother," somewhat louder.
"Glad to hear it. Morgan, come up here."
Red got up and walked to the front of the class.
"You live in Castle Street do you not?"
"Yes Brother."
"Do you know Campbell's shoe shop?"
"Yes Brother."
"Good."
Reaching into his trouser pocket he produced an eighteen inch long black leather strap.
"Take this to Campbell's and have them mend the stitching here," he said pointing to a frayed area of the strap.
"And wait on it."
"Yes Brother."

Red left the class and cut through the Secondary School area which took him out onto Castle Street. A few minutes later he was standing in Campbell's shoe shop.

"Hello young Morgan and what can I do for ya?" greeted Bobby Campbell.

"Brother Feenan wants ya to sew this for him please."

"He does, does he. Let's see then?"

Taking the strap from Red he examined it, turning it over a number of times.

"Hmm, and I suppose he wants it done now, does he?"

"He does."

"Typical, typical…well let's see…"

After another examination Bobby began undoing the stitching with a knife. After he had completed a few inches on either side of the strap he opened it up. Red was watching closely.

"What's that Mr. Campbell?" asked Red pointing to the inside of the strap.

"What…this?" said Bobby, lifting up the centre piece.

"Yeah."

"That's lead son. It makes the strap heavy. All the better for hittin' ya with," he laughed.

"Lead?" asked Red astonished.

"Yep. There's an inch wide strip of it which runs the length of the strap."

"Wow, I never knew that was in there."

Bobby laughed loudly.

"One thing about the Brothers, they know how to inflict pain so they do. Experts at it for sure. It wouldn't surprise me to learn that they took special classes durin' their trainin' on how to beat the boys they teach with some expertise."

Red just swallowed and nodded. It took about fifteen minutes to complete the job on the belt which was duly handed back to him.

"Now make sure young Morgan ya don't give cause to have that used on your own self."

"I won't," answered Red seriously.

After arriving back in the classroom and returning the strap to Brother Feenan, Red took his seat. He was happy to have had the thirty minute break.

"Now…getting back to our Catechism…Hillen…who is God?"
Po was caught off guard. He began to stammer. The black flowing robes of Brother Feenan were closing quickly on his position.
"Ah…God is…is…God is…"
"God is what, Hillen?" shouted Brother Feenan.
"God is…"
"What?" continued Brother Feenan, his voice getting louder.
"I…can't remember Brother," Po managed to get out feebly.
Brother Feenan had a twelve inch wooden ruler in his hand. Using the edge he began hitting Po's head in time with his voice.
"God…is…love…God…is…love…Now what is God?"
"God is love," mumbled Po. Red was staring at him. He saw Po's eyes were filling with tears.
"Again…What is God?"
"God is love."
"Louder," roared Brother Feenan continuing to drum Po's head with the ruler's edge.
"God is love," shouted Po.
"Excellent…excellent."

Later that day Red and Po were sitting in Uncle Luigi's Café with Jumpy Jones and Topcoat Anderson.
"They're all the same, every friggin' one of them, sadistic bastards," commented Topcoat.
"That's for sure, but we can do nothin' about it can we?" said Red.
"When I was at school they were even worse than they are now. They would'a punched ya in the mouth as quick as look at ya," added Topcoat.
"De ya know, the sad part of it all is there's no one ta complain ta. If I went home and told my auld fella that Brother so and so gave me a hidin', he would most likely hit me a scud and tell me I didn't get it for nothin'."

"Mine's the same," added Jumpy.

"There has to be some way we can get our own back on that bastard," said Po thoughtfully.

"What we need is an adult who will back us," said Red.

"Yeah right, ya have some hope. Someone ta stand up ta the Christian Brothers? There's no such person," said Topcoat.

"Red, who do we know that would actually listen to ya?" asked Po.

"I don't know anybody…well other than Dr. Wilson."

"Dr. Wilson?"

"Well he at least listens to ya."

"Ya might have something there…let me think about it."

"He's off on one of his mad plans…I can feel it comin'," laughed Red.

"Well, if anyone can come up with a plan it's Po," said Jumpy.

"Now hold on a mo. Ya mentioned Dr. Wilson there Red. I think I might be gettin' an idea. Jumpy, I want ya ta go ta the library and get me a book on concussion."

"On what?"

"Concussion…never mind…I'll write it down for ya."

"No problem."

"What have ya come up with?" asked Red.

"A real beauty, just wait till I get the whole thing worked out in ma head, ya'll love it."

Red and Po exchanged glances as they took their seats in class. A faint smile of understanding passed between them.

"Now you lot, get your homework out quickly," growled Brother Feenan.

There was movement throughout the class with one exception, Po Hillen. He never moved, just sat there looking at the blackboard. This soon caught the attention of the Brother who quickly moved to Po's desk.

"Where's your homework Hillen?"

"Da da didn't ah da do the homework Brother."

"What?"

"I da, da.."

"What do you mean you didn't do your homework Hillen?"

"Did…didn't da, do it."

"Why didn't you do it?"

"Don't…a…know."

"Get up to the front of the class Hillen."

Po stood up and walked slowly to the front followed by Brother Feenan.

"Well, what have you to say for yourself before I take the hide off you?"

"Don't…a…know…what…ta…say."

"Why are you stammering Hillen?"

"Don't…not…stammerin'… "

"Brother," Red had his hand up.

"What Morgan?"

"Could I speak to ya in private Sir, it's ta do with Hillen?"

"Outside," he beckoned towards the door.

Red left the classroom followed by Brother Feenan.

"Well boy?"

"Sir, he has been acting strange all day yesterday. He was forgettin' things and gettin' confused and as well as that he started stammerin' and his eyes went all funny."

"All day yesterday you say? He was quite normal in class."

"Yeah Brother, I know, but it was shortly after school he started actin' funny and it was then I remembered."

"Remembered what?"

"What I read in one of ma dad's magazines."

"What did you read?"

"It was about a thing called…called…contussion I think."

"Concussion do you mean?"

"That's the word Sir. It said that blows to the head could cause it and the person could have all the symptoms that he has."

"Concussion…well we'd better get him to the Doctor right away just in case."

"Well the piece I read said that's what it was ok, but I don't think it's serious in Hillen's case since he didn't blackout. That's when ya know it's bad Sir."

"We will still have to get him to the doctor in any case."

"But Brother…" Red lowered his voice.

"It could cause an awful lot of trouble so it could."

"Trouble? What are you talking about Morgan?"

"Well Sir, if he has con…"

"Concussion."

"Concussion Sir, the only blows ta the head he got were from you!"

"What?"

"But it's not serious Sir, all he needs is rest and it'll go away."

"I see…I see. Ok, now this is what will be done. You will take him home and tell his parents he wasn't feeling well. Tell them I said he is to take the rest of the week off…understand?"

"Yes Sir."

"Now there is not to be a word of this to anyone Morgan…do you understand…no one?"

"Ya can rely on me Brother."

****

"I have never seen anybody eat chips as fast as you, do ya know that?" Red said to Po as they sat in Uncle Luigi's an hour later.

"I like chips."

"So what, ya don't have ta eat them like ya were starvin'."

"I do, I do."

"My dog eats slower."

"A week's holiday, how about that then?"

"All I got was a friggin' day off."

"Well, are ya complainin'?"

"No."

"Sure ya done a great job, ya should be in the movies."

"I should, you're right, especially with my looks."

Po reached across and placed his hand on Red's forehead.

"Yeah, it's concussion all right."

"Piss off you. We were lucky ta get away with it ya know."

"So what?... I'll bet no one will ever be hit on the head again by that bastard."

"I would take bets on that."

"He'll bate the arse off everyone now that he can't hit us on the head."

"I think ya could be right."

"I wonder is there such a thing as arse concussion?"

Red dropped his head into his hands.
"Jasus help me."

****

"Well it's beginnin' ta look a wee bit tidier at least," said Red's mom standing at the bedroom door. Red was jolted back to the present.
"Well at least ya can see the other side of the floor now. What's that on your cheek? Come over here."
Red walked to where his mom was standing and looked down at her.
"Can ya not even keep your face clean for five minutes, can ya not?" she said producing a handkerchief from her apron pocket.
Red knew what was coming and he hated it with a passion.
"I'll go and wash," he pleaded, but it was too late.
His mom grabbed his chin, spat on the handkerchief, and proceeded to rub the offending mark from his face.
"I hate ya doing that," Red moaned rubbing his face.
"God, you're such a baby. Have ya everythin' put away in its proper place? I don't want ta see things just stuffed in drawers."
"I've hung up some things and put the rest neatly into the drawers."
"Good, well what are ya standin' there for? Get on with it."
"I'll make a deal with ya, you don't spit wash my face again and I will keep my room spotless, deal?"
"Deal," smiled Mrs. Morgan

End

The Canal Crossing

1958

It was a beautiful warm summer's day as Red Morgan, Po Hillen, Shifty McShane and Jumpy Jones made their way along the tow-path of the Newry Canal. They had arranged to meet up with another six of their mates at the large oak tree in the grounds of St. Coleman's College which bordered the canal tow-path.

"I hope they got the rope ok," said Shifty.
"Waste of time if they didn't," answered Red.
As they reached the first lock on the now disused canal, Red stopped.
"I'll cross here and meet you guys at the oak tree, ok?"
Red crossed the walkway on the wooden lock gates to the bank on the other side of the canal. He continued walking for another 300 yards until he was opposite the oak tree.

The rest of the gang was already there. Dunno McManus was in the process of tying a rope around the tree trunk some thirty feet above the ground. When the series of hellos and insults between the two groups and Red were finished, the boys returned to the task. The idea was to string the rope across the canal between the two trees. The end of the rope was finally thrown across to Red who proceeded to climb the tree and tie it level to the other side.

"Right, it's ready," Red shouted to the group on the other side.

"Well, try it Red," shouted back Jumpy Jones.

"Are you wee girls afraid ta go first? Ah, well don't worry, I'll try it for ya."

Red reached out along the rope with his right hand and eased his body weight off the tree. Grabbing the rope with his other hand, he let go of the tree completely and started moving along the rope. He made it look simple as he eased his way across, hand over hand until he had reached the other side.

"There ya go...nothin' to it."

"Nice one Red. Ok, let's get across then," said Jumpy.

Within minutes everyone was on the rope and starting across the canal. Red was still in the tree, laid back on a branch having a smoke. He watched as the clothesline of dangling, twisting bodies slowly made their way across. Strong as the rope was, the weight of nine bobbing bodies was just a little too much. Red was the first to see the rope starting to fray.

"Hey...the rope...!"

Before he could get the warning to the canal crossers, the rope broke! Down they all went screaming and kicking into the beautiful muddy, weedy depths of the Newry Canal.

Red scrambled down the tree as quickly as he could and ran to the bank. By this time the air was filled with a chorus of obscenities that could have been heard in the centre of Newry. First to the bank was Shifty. Red reached out and grabbed his hand.

"Ya bastard Morgan....ya cut the rope!" panted Shifty.

"Pull the bastard in," came the shouts from behind him.

Red, sensing the danger, immediately let Shifty fall backwards into the canal.

"Get him....get him...!" Red could hear the shouts as the gang made their way quickly to the bank. He spun and took off like a greyhound along the canal tow-path. He could hear the split splat of soggy shoes running after him. The pursuers gave up after a few minutes but Red continued until he reached the safety of the town. When he stopped to look back, he saw them all removing muddy shoes and clothing. He could almost hear them trying to outdo each other by shouting the longest single sentence consisting solely of obscenities.

As Red walked through the front door of his home, he met his mother.

"Where were you?"

"Just down at the canal with the boys."

"Did ya have a nice time?"

"Great. But the lads didn't enjoy it too much!"

"Why was that son?"

"They all had too much washin' ta do."

Red's mom gave him a puzzled look. She took a breath as if to ask another question, but had second thoughts, just shook her head and left. As Red walked along the hallway in his house, he had a broad grin on his face. He thought, 'I'll bet that was the first bath some of them buggers had this month!'

End

The Cup Match

1958

Uncle Luigi's was bustling with Newry Town FC supporters when Red Morgan arrived that Saturday. It was the usual meeting place for Red and his mates before all the home games, but this Saturday was a very special day and had been awaited with anticipation by every football fan in the Newry area. The visitors this week were the Irish League Champions, Linfield. Newry was only a 'B' Division team, but always kept the dream alive of one day reaching the dizzy heights of the Irish League.

"Yo Red," came a voice from behind. Turning, he could see the smiling face of Po Hillen who seemed to be covered from head to toe in the Newry Town colours of blue and white. Red simply wore his Newry scarf tied around his neck.

"The big day has arrived," announced Po.

"Where's the rest of the mob?"

"They're all here, out back with Anto."

"We will kick Belfast arses today."

"I hope so."

"Three nil, you wait!"

"I couldn't care less about the score, just as long as we win. Po, don't forget, they don't win the Irish League almost every year by bein' a shitty team ya know."

"Ah sure that's only because we're not in the Irish League."

"Aye, right."

An hour later, Red, Po, and eight more of the gang were positioned in their usual place behind the goal. The Marshes, or to give it its proper title, The Showgrounds, was the home of Newry Town FC. Both teams were now on the pitch warming up. The heckling had already begun between the two sets of supporters. The Linfield followers were in the 'Old Stand' and already through their second rendering of 'The Sash'. They knew the song got up the noses of the vast majority of Newry supporters who came from Nationalist backgrounds.

The shrill sound of the referee's whistle brought the game to life as both sets of supporters tried their best to out-sing and out-cheer each other. By half-time neither team had scored. Being able to hold the mighty Linfield was, in fact, a moral victory for Newry.

"I'm gonna get some drink," said Jumpy Jones to no one in particular.

"They won't serve ya in there," commented Po.

"I know one of the barmen, he promised ta slip me some drink out the back door."

Fifteen minutes later the second half had begun and Jumpy was back with a half bottle of John Powers Whiskey which he had already started on with some enthusiasm.

Midway through the second half one of the Newry forwards was tripped and taken down inside the Linfield penalty area. The referee immediately pointed to the spot. The Newry supporters were ecstatic and drowned out the boos from the Linfield crowd. Jimmy Edgar, the Newry centre forward stepped up and calmly put the ball out of the goalkeeper's reach into the back of the net to give Newry a 1- 0 lead.

By this time Jumpy Jones was feeling the effects of the whiskey. He could hardly stand!

"Red, what'll we do with Jumpy? The moron is out of his tree," said Dunno.

"Well, if he stays here he'll end up gettin' trampled at the end of the match."

"Take him out ta the car park and let him sleep there till after the match," suggested Anto.

"Good idea, grab an arm," said Bishop Keenan.

The Bishop, with the help of Dunno dragged a now mumbling, incoherent Jumpy out of the ground. Some 10 minutes later they were back without Jumpy.

"Where did ya put him?" asked Po.

"We put him in the back seat of one a the buses ta keep him safe ta later."

"Nice one."

The referee looked at his watch, placed the whistle in his mouth, and gave three short blows. It was all over. Newry Town had done it. They had beaten the mighty Linfield. The Newry supporters were elated and streamed onto the pitch.

As Red and the gang were slowly making their way back up the Warrenpoint Road toward the town, the conversation was of the great feat of the Newry Team and how they would fare in the next round. Bishop Keenan suddenly stopped.

"Jasus Christ."

"What?" asked Red, looking at the Bishop.

"Friggin' Jumpy!"

"Shit, we forgot all about him, we'll have ta go back," said Po.

"Stupid, dumb bastard," muttered Red as they all turned and hurried back towards the Showgrounds. When they reached the car park, all the buses were gone.

"What do we do now?" asked Dunno.

"We'd better have a look around just ta be sure," said Red.

They spread out, and searched the car park and inside the ground… no Jumpy!

"Red, ya don't think he's still on the bus, do ya?"

"It's possible, where else could he be?"

"What bus did ya put him on?" Red asked the Bishop.

"Shit I don't know, it was just a bus, and it was open."

"Not just a bus, Bishop," said a worried Red, "could it have been a Linfield bus?"

"Oh Christ, he'll end up in Belfast," Po spurted out.

"Bishop, think carefully, did he have a Newry scarf on him?" asked Red.

"No, I took his scarf, he didn't need it, the state he was in," said Dunno.

"Well at least they won't know he's a Newry supporter if he stays asleep," said Red. "He could end up sleepin' all the way ta Belfast."

"That's if he reaches Belfast a'tall," said the Bishop rubbing his chin.

"What'll we do?" asked Naffy McKay who'd been quiet until now.

"There's nothin' we can do!" said Red. "Let's meet in Uncle Luigi's at eight o'clock. If he hasn't turned up by then, we'll have ta come up with a plan of action."

They all agreed.

That night the gang had gathered in Uncle Luigi's.

"Any word?" asked Red who was the last to arrive.

"Nothin'! I called ta his house on the way here and he's not there," said Blackie Havern.

The next half hour was spent debating.

"Should we not tell his da?" asked Dunno.

"What are ya gonna say Dunno? We put him on a bus ta sleep it off cause he was pissed?" asked Anto sarcastically.

"Shit," spurted out Po, "it's friggin' Jumpy," pointing at the door.

Jumpy Jones had just walked in looking no worse for wear.

"Where the hell were you?" asked Red

"I was in friggin' Belfast," slurred Jumpy as he sat down.

"What happened?" everyone seemed to ask at the same time.

Anto arrived with a steaming cup of hot coffee. "Get on the outside of that."

Every one had gathered around Jumpy, to ask questions.

"When did ya wake up?"

"Where'd the bus go?"

"Did they know ya were from Newry?"

"How did ya get back home?"

"Tell us the story."

"Will ya all shut up for Christ's sake? My head's burstin'," muttered Jumpy.

"Well, tell us then!" said Po.

"Well, it was like this. I heard loads of voices and I sorta woke up. Someone was tellin' me ta move over. It suddenly dawned on me that I was on a bus and it was movin'. I sorta didn't give a shit at the time, I was still sorta drunk I think."

"When did ya wake up again?" said Dunno.

"Will ya let me tell the story?"

"Let him tell the story Dunno, shut up!" they all seemed to say together.

"Don't know how long I was sleepin' but I remember openin' my eyes and seein' loads of red, white and blue scarves and hats, so I started to panic. I knew I was on a Linfield bus but couldn't figure how I got there."

"That was the brains of the year, Dunno and Bishop," smirked Po.

"I looked out the window and saw I was comin' inta Belfast and I thought I'd better get off this friggin' bus before someone starts askin' questions."

"So…what did ya do?" asked Anto impatiently.

"Anto," came the chorus.

"All right, all right, I'll shut up."

"Well, everyone around me just left me alone knowin' I was drunk so I decided ta stay drunk as far as they were concerned. I got up and started ta stagger up the centre of the bus. 'Hi fella,' someone said, 'Are ya all right?' As a said, a decided ta play at being very drunk and hopin' a could pass off as a Proddy like the rest of them. I just shouted 'Kick the Pope!' They all started cheerin' and clappin' me on the back like I was one of them. I got ta the bus driver and told him I wanted off, so he stopped. We were at the King's Hall by now. I waved goodbye ta everyone on the bus and got off again shoutin' 'Frig the Pope!' I got another great cheer with loads of wavin' and stuff as the bus drove off. I then started hitchin' back towards Newry and got a lift in a lorry that was headin' for Dublin, and that's the whole story."

"Holy shit, you were one lucky bastard," commented Anto.
"Lucky? I'd say blessed!" added Po.

The next half hour was spent going over and over all the details of the story. Finally Jumpy stood up and announced his intention to go home and get some sleep.
"Well lads, see ya all tomorrow," he stopped on his way out and turned back towards the gang who were still sitting around the table.
"Hi," he shouted. Everyone looked around. "God Save the Queen!"
Jumpy disappeared out the door followed by a hail of language that one would not normally expect to hear from Newry Town Supporters!

End

Fright Night

1958

All the cleaning was done in Uncle Luigi's Café that Friday night. The doors were locked, and the usual crowd was sitting in the front snug eating their fish and chips.

"Look, at least a third of the people in this town will tell ya they've seen a ghost. They can't all be makin' it up."

"That's not the point Anto, ya never hear of anybody our age who's seen one. They're always auld ones who'll tell ya that," said Jumpy Jones.

"Jumpy's right, anyway I don't believe in all that shit, it's all in their minds," commented Red.

"Oh, will ya listen to Mister know it all, you're like all the rest Red. You claim there's no such thing as ghosts or spirits, but that's only in company. I'd bet on your own in the dark, somewhere creepy, it would be a different story," said Anto, his index finger almost at Red's chest.

"Listen Anto, do ya think I'm stupid. I know what you're at. You're tryin' ta set me up ya bastard, but it won't work. You're wastin' your time."

"No way Red, I'm just statin' a fact. Now, as for me, I'm like you, I don't believe in all that shit either, but I wouldn't be in a graveyard at this time of night on my own for any money, would you?"

"Well, ta tell ya the truth, it wouldn't bother me."

"Ach Red, don't talk shit. You know friggin' well ya wouldn't walk through a graveyard at night on your own."

At this point, Dunno McManus and Jumpy Jones stood up to leave.

"You wee girls can talk about bogey men all night till ya wet your knickers, we're off home."

There were now only three left, Anto, Red and Shifty McShane. Anto started back at Red.

"Where was I? Right, as a was sayin', there's no way ya would not be shakin' in yer knickers in a graveyard on your own at night, a know I would."

"You're wastin' your time Anto, whatever you've planned, I'm not bitin'."

"Listen Red, I'm just havin' a conversation, I haven't planned anythin'… honest."

"I agree with Anto," added Shifty. "I wouldn't be in a graveyard at night on my own, and I don't believe in ghosts either."

"For Christ's sake, sure that makes no sense. If ya don't believe in ghosts, what would ya be afraid of?"

"Well, that's the point, a don't know what I'd be afraid of. All a know is a would be," said Anto.

"Look, I'm not boastin', but it wouldn't bother me in the slightest," said Red.

The word 'shit' was used by both Anto and Shifty.

"Look, some night I'll prove it ta ya, no bother."

"Right Red, some night, some week, some year, sometime never, we know."

"Well, we can't do it tonight, it's too late and there'd be no way ta prove you actually did it," said Shifty.

"True, but I'll do it this week, ok?"

"Hang on a minute, I can find out if he did it Anto," spurted out Shifty.

"How?"

"I'm goin' to a funeral in the mornin' after eight o'clock Mass. Johnny Feron is bein' buried."

"So what?"

"Sure I'm a genius. Give Red somethin' belongin' to ya, like a hankie, right? I can tell him where Johnny's bein' buried cause his family grave is next ta ma aunt's. The grave'll be open now for the funeral. When I go up there in the mornin' I'll know if he's been there!"

"What de ya think Red?" asked Anto.

"Sounds ok to me, I'll go there tonight, it's only a little outta ma way, won't bother me in the slightest."

"Right," said Anto as he produced a white handkerchief from his pocket. Taking a pen, he wrote his initials on the hankie.

"Here, drop this in the grave before the bogey man gets ya," laughed Anto handing Red the handkerchief.

"Right, smart ass, see ya tomorrow."

Red and Shifty left and walked the length of Hill Street together before Shifty turned off in the direction of the Dromalane housing estate, where he lived. Red walked the half mile down the Warrenpoint Road until he reached the graveyard. It was a clear, warm night with a full moon lighting up a cloudless summer sky. He remembered Shifty's directions to the grave. After climbing over the wall he walked toward the site. Five minutes later he was standing at an open grave. The soil was piled to one side in readiness for the burial the next morning. He looked around the graveyard. There was total silence broken only by the sound of an owl hooting in the distance. 'Ghosts, those guys talk some shit' he mused. He looked around and selected a small rock, wrapped the handkerchief around it and moved to the mouth of the open grave to drop it in. Suddenly a loud noise shattered the peace of the surroundings.

"Ohooo."

Red felt as if an electric shock had gone through his entire body. He stared, eyes fixed in the direction of the noise which seemed to be coming from the open grave. Just then a white glowing figure began slowly rising from the opening, the sound still ringing in his ears.

"Ohooo."

Red's whole body reacted. He spun around and bolted in the direction of the Warrenpoint Road. Rather than wait until he reached the wall, Red lunged through the hedge. He was now on the Warrenpoint Road and ran an additional hundred yards before he stopped. Bent forward with his hands on his knees he heard a familiar voice.

"Ya know, ya need ta stop smokin' Red. It's slowin' ya down somethin' dreadful."

On a bench about 10 yards away sat Anto and Shifty.

"What the…" mumbled Red still trying to find his breath.

Suddenly from behind he heard a second voice.

"Lovely night for a stroll."

Spinning around he recognized the two approaching figures of Dunno McManus and Jumpy Jones. It all began to register now in Red's mind.

"Bastards, friggin' dirty rotten bastards, I knew it, in the back of ma mind I knew it."

The still night air was filled with the laughter of the gang, that is, all except Red who was now sitting on the bench beside Anto and Shifty, his head in his hands, still breathing heavily.

"I can't believe I let ya sucker me Anto, ya bastard, I'll get ya for this, I swear it."

"Ach Red, now, don't be like that. Sure look at all the trouble we went to just for you?"

"That's right, me and Jumpy had ta borrow this sheet and I had ta swipe our fella's new torch, and all just for you!"

"And what thanks do we get?" asked Jumpy looking at Anto.

"None, none a'tall," answered Anto seriously.

"Come on, we might as well go home, we're just not appreciated ya know."

"No appreciation, you're right, what's this world comin' ta?"

"Yis are a bunch of bastards, I'll get ya all back, ya friggin' just wait," panted Red.

They walked back up the Warrenpoint Road toward Newry. The conversation was subdued but the word 'bastards' could be distinctly heard in the still of that summer night.

End

The Confession

1958

"A sixpence?"

"Ah come on Po, it's all I've got," pleaded Lanky Larkin.

"You've no chance Lanky, two bob's the limit, ya know that."

Lanky shuffled off mumbling to himself.

It was six o'clock on that Saturday in Uncle Luigi's Café. The place was bustling with weekend shoppers loaded with parcels and just too tired to go home and cook. Po had devised an ingenious way of making some money for the weekend. He was taking bets on the Saturday night Confessions in the Cathedral. Everyone was under threat from their parents to go every week, but very, very few ever did.

Po's idea was to time everyone who placed a bet. Whoever stayed in the confessional the longest won the pot. Quite simple and yet, quite effective. So far Po had taken in £7.4s in bets. Everyone was sure they were going to win. Even Red was persuaded to bet. Anto knew he would win. He was convinced he had a brilliant string of sins to confess that would keep him in the confessional all night. Red too had some good ideas but he also had a feeling that Po was up to something!

The moment had arrived. It was seven-thirty in the evening. The whole gang was sitting in the pews outside the first Confession Box on the right hand side of the church. They had information that a priest, new to the parish, would be using this box. When the priest arrived, he stopped short of the confessional and stared at the gang now numbering more than ten who waited solemnly outside his confessional. He looked around nervously at the other three confessionals in operation. A sprinkling of people was divided among them. As if getting courage from Heaven, he looked up, took a deep breath and entered the box.

"Right," whispered Po. "Ya all have your numbers. I'll do the timin'. "
Po had come prepared. He had his jotter and pen, and a stopwatch. The first penitent was Jumpy Jones. He lasted a full four minutes and seven seconds. Next was Boots Markey, then Kitter Murray and so on until everyone had confessed. Red had a respectable time of five minutes and eleven seconds. Anto, who thought he was certain to win, could only manage five minutes and two seconds. Po handed the stop watch to Red. "Now, no messin' Red. Keep the time and write it down, ok?"
"Promise…no messin', I'll do it right."
Red started the stop watch as Po closed the door of the confessional behind him. A conversation started with everyone checking their times. What seemed a short time later, Red glanced at the watch. His eyes widened when he realized that Po had already been in the box for nine minutes! When the door of the confessional opened and Po stepped out, Red looked at the watch as he stopped the second hand. Twelve minutes twenty two seconds! He could not believe it. Po had won by a mile.

"Come on tell me ya wee weasel?" Red pressured when they were on their own and heading home.
"No."
"Tell me?"
"No."
"I'll get ya a date with Cathy Kearns."
"No."

"Tell me what ya want then?"

"Nothin'. "

"Po, now I'm your very best mate, and ya know…"

"No."

"Bastard."

"Shithead."

"Ah! Come on Po, I'd tell you."

Po stopped and looked at Red.

"If I tell ya, you'll tell everyone and I'll never be able ta use it again."

"Look, I promise I'll keep it ta myself. After all, next time ya try it I'll bet on ya and make a fortune."

"Ok then…guess."

Red looked at the evening sky.

"You murdered somebody?"

"Don't be stupid."

"You raped a goat?"

"No, but that's worth keepin' in mind, not bad."

"All right, I give up, what did ya tell the poor priest?"

"Jumpy Jones."

"What?"

"I told him about Jumpy Jones."

"What about Jumpy Jones?"

"I told him I was swimmin' in the canal with Jumpy and I was gettin' feelin's for him."

"Whaddya mean?"

"I told him I was gettin' a hard on lookin' at Jumpy Jones."

"You told the priest ya think you're a fruit?"

"Yep."

Red spun around and slapped his head letting out a roar.

"Ya crafty wee bastard. Ya sneaky wee frigger. Ya…"

"All right, all right, don't get carried away."

"You're a genius. I wouldn't have thought a that in a million years."

"What can I tell ya?" said Po with a satisfied, ear to ear, grin.

They walked on for a few minutes talking about the penance the priest gave Po. When they reached the point where they separated for their homes, Red stopped and looked at Po.

"Can I ask ya somethin'?"

"All jokin' aside now, right?"

"Right."

"I mean, like, will I be safe goin' for a swim with ya in the future?"

Red had always been a good runner. It took fifty yards before he lost a red faced screaming Po.

End

The Grave Question

1960

Po Hillen and Red Morgan were walking along Castle Street one sunny summer morning.

"Look, this is what happens, they take the body out and put it somewhere else," said Po.

"Now you are being ridiculous," snapped Red.

They had just reached Red's house. He opened the door and they both entered and walked down the long hallway until they reached the kitchen where they found Red's grandmother cooking.

"Granny, can I ask you a question about the graveyard?" asked Red.

"Ya don't talk about graveyards to an old person," she smiled.

Red and Po giggled.

"Seriously, we have been having this argument ya see. Now suppose a family lose two people, like they die, and they are buried side by side in the grave, right? Now, six months later another member of the family dies."

"Not having a lot of luck that family," smiled Granny Morgan.

"Now, does this mean that the coffin will only be buried four feet down? Or do they, as Po says, remove one of the other coffins?"

Granny Morgan rubbed her chin.

"Ya know, ta be honest, I never gave that any thought a'tall. Where do ya come up with these questions?"

"I think they have to remove one of the coffins so they do. The law says a coffin must be buried six feet down. Now, if they put the coffin on top of another one, they would be breakin' the law, cause it would only be four feet down, and sure what if there were three people died the second time? That means that one of the coffins would be only two feet down?" stated Po.

"Lads, I have no idea a'tall. Ya better ask your dad when he comes in," laughed Granny Morgan.

Both left the house and retraced their steps back to the centre of Newry and to Uncle Luigi's Café. There were very few customers in at this time so Anto Falsoni, who was working behind the chip counter, joined Red and Po in the first snug.

"Well, did Granny Morgan know anythin' about the graves?" said Anto as he sat down.

"She had no idea," answered Po.

"So who can we ask?" asked Anto.

"A priest?" suggested Po.

"Are ya out a your skull, no way," snapped Red.

"There might be a way," mused Anto rubbing his chin.

"Wow Anto, I'm not diggin' up any friggin' graves, that's for sure," said Red seriously.

Anto and Po both laughed at Red's seriousness.

"No ya auld ejit, I have another idea," said Anto.

"Go on," said Red.

"A was thinkin' about those long thin steel rods out the back that are for locking the veg cages together. They screw together so they do and ya can make them any length ya want."

"Jasus, I hope you're not thinkin' what I think you're thinkin'?" said Red in a serious voice.

"Why not, we can do it at night, who would know? It's simple."

"Will one of you two tell me what the hell yis are talkin' about," asked Po.

"Look, that ejit is suggesting we go ta the graveyard in the middle of the night and push or hammer a steel rod into a grave ta see how deep the coffin is," answered Red.

"Jasus Anto, that's a brilliant idea," said Po with a broad grin.

"If ya were caught ya would end up in jail for sure," warned Red.

"No way Red, we're not digging up a grave or causing any damage, just making a wee small hole that will fill when we take the rod out," explained Anto.

"Yeah, suppose you're right," admitted Red.

"When will we do it?" asked a smiling excited Po.

"Wow not so fast, we need ta work this out carefully. We need ta know which grave ta go ta," said Anto.

"How will we know that?" asked Red.

"Find out who was last buried and where," answered Anto.

"Got ya," smiled Po.

Three days later after investigations and visits to the graveyard, the boys met in Uncle Luigi's Café once again.

"Right, here is the info," said Po handing Anto a crumpled piece of paper.

"Billy McFearon from Dromalane Park was buried on Tuesday last. Red and I made a map of where the grave is."

"Yeah, this will be easy ta get to. We can get over the wall in the middle of Chapel Hill," said Anto.

"So when do we go?"

"I think tomorra' night would be good, ya ok with that Red?"

"Sounds ok ta me."

"Po?"

"Great, will we meet here?"

"Right, now tell nobody, agreed?" said Anto seriously.

Red and Po both nodded and mumbled agreement.

As the three made their way up Chapel Street towards the graveyard there was little talk. It was a bright moonlit night, and very quiet. They had passed no one since leaving the Café. The moon was low in the sky causing long shadows. Po's earlier excitement had somehow waned, Red had noticed him glancing around.

"Looking for ghosts are ya Po?" smiled Red.

"Frig off Morgan," snapped Po.

Red laughed.

"Ya see Anto, Po is afraid of things that go bump in the night," said Red as he suddenly grabbed Po, who jumped and pulled away.

"Ya're a friggin' bastardin', whorin' fruit, and a hope ya never find who your da was," snarled Po.

Red and Anto went into fits of laughter.

"Not friggin' funny shit faces."

They soon reached the part of the graveyard wall they had planned to climb over. All three were over quickly and began the search for the grave.

"Here it is," whispered Po as he stopped and pointed at a headstone.

"Ya sure?" whispered Anto.

"Yeah, that's it ok."

"Look, see where the soil is soft, and the fresh flowers, that's where they buried him so it is," said Po.

"Red, you're stronger than me, you take the rod and try it," said Anto.

"Are ya afraid wee Anto?" mocked a smiling Red.

"Piss off and take it will ya?"

Red took the rod, he moved some of the flowers out of his way, and found a spot to begin pushing the rod through the soft soil.

"Po, give us a hand will ya."

Po moved opposite Red and took hold of the rod with both hands.

"Right, here we go," said Red.

Lifting the pole off the ground he rammed it down into the soil. The silence of the night was shattered by Po's scream.

"What? What?" Red exclaimed.

"Ya nearly put the whorin' thing through ma whorin' friggin' foot so ya did," Po managed to get out while he hopped around on one leg holding the injured foot.

Anto sympathetically sat down at the side of the grave and roared with laughter. Red joined him.

"It's not funny ya bastards, a could be crippled for life so a could."

This in no way helped the situation, if anything, it made it worse. Red was now lying on his side on the ground and Anto was leaning on top of him.

Some ten minutes later, the laughter was reduced to sobs and coughing, tears being wiped, sides being rubbed.
"Ok, right, let's try this again. Now Po, keep your voice down will ya, the screams of ya, for God's sake, ya would waken the dead."
This was too much for Anto, he was off again, on the ground rolling. Red now realised what he had said and joined Anto. It took almost five minutes for them to settle down and get back to the task in hand.

"Will ya push will ya Po?" whispered Red.
"How far down is it now?" queried Anto.
"I think about three feet," answered Po.
"Right we'll need the hammer now Anto," said Red.
Anto reached into his inside pocket and produced a claw hammer. He handed it to Red.

****

"Jasus, that fella can throw pints down," said Charlie Rafferty.
"That he can. One mouthful and it's gone," slurred Butty Craven.
The two were on their way home to the Warrenpoint Road after leaving their local, Murther's Public House on Castle Street.
Both men were in their middle sixties and with their age and the amount of Guinness consumed, progress was quite slow, and not always in a straight line. They were halfway down Chapel Hill, just a few hundred yards from their destination.
"I hate this friggin' road so I do," mumbled Butty looking around.
"So do I, friggin' creepy so it is."
"People have seen things here ya know," whispered Butty.
"I know. I heard that last year Biff Toner was walkin' down here and saw a man whose funeral he was at a week earlier, standing at the graveyard wall, nearly killed him so it did. He's never been the same since."

"Jasus. That was somethin'. This road is the creepiest road I have ever been on in ma life so it is. If you're ever goin' ta see a ghost, this is where it'll be."

Suddenly the stillness of the night was shattered by a shrill scream coming from the graveyard just over the wall opposite them. Both men stopped dead in their tracks. It was as if a bolt of electricity had gone through their bodies.

Without a word, they took off at speed breathlessly relating prayers.

"Jesus Mary and Joseph, help me."

Old age, alcohol, aches and pains, were all forgotten as the two raced down Chapel Hill doing a fair impression of Olympic Sprinters.

****

"How far down now Red?" asked Anto.

Red produced a tape measure from his pocket and measured the rod.

"It's just over four feet."

"Ok, should be nearly there."

Red was tapping the rod with the hammer, he had covered the top with a handkerchief to abate the noise. Suddenly the rod hit something solid. Red tapped a little more and felt the vibration travel up the rod.

"This is it. I've hit something solid. This must be the coffin for sure."

"Jasus, great stuff, now measure it Red," said an excited Anto.

Red did so.

"I make it four feet eleven inches," said Red.

"Can we go now?" asked Po softly.

"Yeah, let's get outta here," said Red.

When they got back onto Chapel Street Anto was the first to speak.

"Well the grave was one foot and an inch too shallow."

"Yeah, it was," said Red.

"So? What have we proven?" asked Po.

"Well we know that either the gravedigger was a lazy bastard or there are coffins in there just a couple of feet under the ground."

"But wouldn't people notice at the burial?" asked Po.

"Naw, they're not stupid these gravediggers ya know. They take the old coffins outta the grave before the burial and hide them outta sight ya see. Then when everyone has gone they put the old coffins back on top of the new one and cover it all up."

"Very smart," commented Red. "By the way, these rods are stinkin' so they are."

"What do ya smell on them?" laughed Anto.

Red held a rod to his face.

"Jasus, like raw meat."

"Great nose ya have there Morgan. I had ta move the uncooked burgers that were sitting on these ones in the freezer."

"They stink to high heaven so they do."

Two days later Red and Anto were sitting in a snug in Uncle Luigi's Cafe sipping their Cokes when an excited breathless Po arrived at the table.

"Look, Jasus, look?" he threw the Newry Reporter down on the table.

Red and Anto looked at the headline Po indicated.

'Police Seek Grave Robbers.'

"Holy shit," exclaimed Anto leaning back.

Red kept reading the full article.

"Wait ya friggin' ejits, did ya read it all?" smiled Red.

"What?" asked Po sliding into the snug.

"Listen," Red began reading.

'At first glance police thought they were looking for grave robbers that appeared to be disturbed before they could finish their work. According to a spokesman, it was later discovered that dogs may have caused the damage to the grave.'

"I don't understand," puzzled Anto.

"Me neither," said Po.

Red was smiling.

"Your smelly rods ya ejit."

"What?" asked Anto with a puzzled look.

"Don't ya see it? All the poking and pushing of the rods, left a smell of meat on the ground. Dogs would have smelled that a thousand yards away, and began diggin'."

"Shit, he's right," exclaimed Po.

"Jasus, I don't mind tellin' yis, I was a bit worried there," said Anto breathing deeply.

Red rubbed his chin.

"Well Anto, I wouldn't say ya were outta the woods yet."

"What de ya mean?" asked Anto, alertness back in his voice.

"Ya could still be arrested ya know," answered Red standing and moving to the front of the snug.

"How, how?" pleaded Po.

"Well, don't ya know, it's a crime ta incite animals ta commit crime."

Po and Anto failed in their mission to catch Red who was out the front door before they were even out of the snug.

So the whole story ended with Butty Craven and Charlie Rafferty having pint buying audiences for many months, two dogs who smelled dinner but never got it, a newspaper whose headline sold thousands more copies, police who had to investigate a two foot hole in a grave, a gravedigger who had to refill it, and Red, Po and Anto who found, through hard and diligent planning, that all bodies were not where they were supposed to be.

End

Cowboys and Indians

1958

It was just past one o'clock as the five made their way towards Ginger Devine's house on the Ballyholland Road, in Newry. His dad was one of the few people in 1958 who owned a television set. The boys were boisterous and filled with anticipation as they climbed the steep hill of High Street on their way to watch the FA Cup Final between Aston Villa and Manchester United. Interest in the cup final was always high in Newry, but more so this year because local footballer, Peter McParland, was playing outside left for Aston Villa.

"Six nil to Villa, six nil to Villa," sang Shifty McShane.
"Three nil to United," sang Lanky Larkin.

They finally reached Devines and settled down to watch the preliminaries before kick off. After ninety minutes of cheering, booing, dancing and screaming, a long blow on the referee's whistle sent the room into raptures. Not only did Aston Villa win the FA Cup two goals to nil, but Newry man, Peter McParland, scored both goals.

The group spilled from the television room into the back garden where, after ten minutes of match replays, it was decided to play a game of 'Cowboys and Indians'. Devine's house backed onto a large wood which was ideal for the game at hand. The group, now swollen to eight, divided in two after the usual arguments of who wanted to be a Cowboy and who wanted to be an Indian.

The game plan was for the Indians to attack the Cowboy camp. Everyone took their places and the game began with the Indians, led by Po, who was Chief Sitting Bull, swooping down on the Cowboy camp with much whooping matched by shooting sounds from the Cowboys. After a prolonged and ferocious battle the Indians were pushed back and Chief Sitting Bull was captured in a devastating blow to his side. A rope was found and the prisoner was tied to a tree. The Cowboys then set off after the remaining Indians. During the ensuing battle, a voice was heard coming from the back door and it stopped everyone in their tracks.

"Boys, come on now, lemonade and buns, hurry up," invited Mrs. Devine.

All hostilities stopped immediately and the group raced into the house. After everything eatable and drinkable had disappeared the boys decided to go home.

On the way back down High Street the match was again replayed in detail. Every foul, every wide, every cross was discussed. When they reached the bottom of High Street the group began to split up and the boys went off in separate directions. Red arrived home full of excitement to find his father, grandfather, and two uncles discussing the match which they had been listening to on the radio. They questioned Red about the goals and how they looked on television; about the near misses, the fouls, and many other details of the game. The group had talked for almost an hour when there was a knock at the front door.

"I'll get it," shouted Red to his mom. He walked down the long hall and opened the door. Standing outside was Po's younger brother, Paul.

"Mom says to tell Po to come for his tea, now."

"Po? He's not here."

"Where is he?"

"Don't know, I thought he went home."

"Well, he didn't so if you see him tell him he's in big trouble."

"Ok, right."

Red closed the door and began walking back down the hall. Half way, he stopped.

'Jasus, he's still tied to the friggin' tree,' Red remembered.

He shouted into the house.

"Be back soon, have ta go out a message."

Some fifteen minutes later Red was racing through the trees to where the Cowboy camp was located. Po was there and still tied to the tree.

"Where were ya, ya bastard?"

Red set Po free to a constant barrage of insults.

"Friggin' bastards, whores, shitheads, morons, I could a been here all night. I could a died or worse."

"Will ya shut up, didn't I come back for ya, didn't I?"

"Oh yeah, ya did, ya bastard, five hours later."

"Po, it's only been an hour."

"An hour? Shit, it was at least five; I could a been eaten by animals or somethin'."

"Naw, they would'a been too afraid of poisonin'."

"Oh very funny…bastard."

By the time they reached the bottom of High Street Red had heard every swear word in the English language. He couldn't understand Po's anger. It wasn't as if it was raining, or snowing. All he missed was a bun and a glass of lemonade. 'Some people are very, very weird' Red thought!

End

Revenge

1959

"So, we can all stay over then?" asked Po through a broad grin.

"Yeah," answered Red as they both walked along Hill Street.

"Shit, we'll have a ball, is everyone goin'?"

"All five of us."

"When are we leavin'?"

"Po, I must 'a told ya this five times already, Saturday mornin' at eleven from Uncle Luigi's."

"Whose caravan is it anyway?"

"Roberto's."

"Anto's uncle?"

"Yeah, he's had it on a permanent site at the Caravan Park in Newcastle for years."

"Is it a big one?"

"Well, I had no complaints so far."

"The caravan, shithead."

"I think it sleeps eight."

"How'd Anto get Roberto ta let him use it?"

"Anto says he had ta promise the earth. That's as much as he'd say, no details."

"How are we gettin' there?"

"Anto organised somebody to take us there and pick us up."

"I can't wait. Hi Red, will I need ta bring a suitcase?"

"Sure ya will, after all, we'll be stayin' for all a one day and one night. You'd need at least ten changes of clothes."

"Don't be a smartarse Morgan, ya know what I mean. What'll I bring? What are you takin'?"

"I'm just takin' what I'm wearin' and one change. But you'll need a suitcase anyway."

"Why?"

"Well, your change of clothes, your Winnie the Pooh pyjamas, your Teddy bears, your…"

"Who told ya I had Winnie the Pooh pyjamas?" snapped Po stopping to grab Red's arm.

"So, ya do have Winnie the Pooh pyjamas then?"

"I didn't say that."

"As much as."

"Who said it?"

"Ya want me ta give up my sources?"

"Ya didn't just make it up outta the blue, that's for sure."

"Ya never know."

"Who said it Morgan?"

"Told ya, can't say, sworn ta silence."

"Get stuffed then."

"You offerin'?"

Po knew he was fighting a losing battle, so he just gave up.

Saturday arrived and all five of the gang were sitting in the front snug in Uncle Luigi's Cafe. There was Po, Anto, Naffy, Jumpy and Red. They were all set for the great adventure. Permission from parents had been sought and granted; major promises were made on Bibles, grandmother's graves, relative's lives; threats were issued and fingers wagged.

Anto had asked another one of his uncles, Tony, to drive them all to Newcastle. Tony, known as 'Big Tony', probably due to the fact that he weighed around twenty-two stone, arrived about eleven-thirty. After much pushing and shoving, squeezing and swearing, they were all in the Vauxhall Cresta and on their way.

Newcastle is twenty miles from Newry on the east coast of Northern Ireland and is a typical seaside town with the main street being equally divided with Chip Shops, Bars, Restaurants, Bed and Breakfasts, Amusement Arcades and Souvenir Shops.

Big Tony pulled into the Mourne Vista Caravan Park and found his way along the dirt road to Roberto's caravan. It was well kept and had a nice little garden at the front with a small picket fence and gate. In no time the boys were inside and settled. All the arguments about who would sleep where were resolved. Caravan equipment had been inspected, touched, wowed at, or groaned about.

Some twenty minutes later the lads were walking along the seafront enjoying the summer sunshine and admiring the groups of young ladies that seemed to be plentiful. The day was spent on the beach, building sand castles, lying in the sun, whispering about the girls who passed in swimsuits, playing football and, of course, swimming.

It was almost eight o'clock when the gang was making its way back to the caravan park…eating fish and chips out of newspaper wrappings.

"Hi Red, how about gettin' some booze?" asked Jumpy
"Sounds like an idea."
"There's a pub," chimed in Po.
"How much can we put together then?" asked Red.
Everyone began rummaging through pockets and it was finally agreed that ten shillings was the amount that could be raised.
"You'll have to go in and get it Red," said Anto. "You look the oldest."
"Ok, so what'll I get?"
"Carling Black Label."
"No way, get Harp."
"Get a grip, Guinness is the only drink to get."
"That stuff's shit, get whiskey."

"Wow, hold on. I'm not gettin' a load of different drinks. Find somethin' ya can all drink."
After much debate it was decided to get pint bottles of Bass.

Red had no problems getting the drink and soon they were back at the caravan drinking Bass and having a good time. Red noticed that Jumpy Jones was getting drunk. He turned to Anto who was sitting beside him.
"Jumpy can't drink a'tall can he?"
"Last year I gave him a drink out back of the café and he fell asleep after one glass," laughed Anto. Red laughed and thought, 'I will get ya tonight, Jones, for the night ya got me at the graveyard. Now, it's my turn'.

An hour and a half later, Red and Po were the only ones still awake. Anto was fast asleep on the sofa and the other two were in the single beds at the back of the caravan. Red told Po what he was going to do. He decided to wait for a while to make sure Jumpy was well into the land of nod. He and Po sat and talked for almost an hour. Eventually, Red stood up and motioned for Po to follow. They quietly entered the room where Jumpy and Naffy were and found both fast asleep. Red edged along Jumpy's bed and gently reaching over pulled back the bedclothes. All Jumpy was wearing was a pair of underpants. Red very gently began to slide Jumpy's underpants down. Po had to keep both his hands over his mouth to stop the giggling from being heard. Red occasionally gave him a stern 'keep quiet' look.

Red pointed at Jumpy's penis and nodded to Po.
"No friggin' way," whispered Po.
"Just lift it up, Po."
"No chance,"
"Po!"
"No," Po said louder.
Jumpy stirred a little. Red motioned Po out of the room.
They both left quietly. Red closed the door gently behind them.
Po was first to speak.
"There's no way I'm touchin' Jumpy Jones's dick."

"Po don't be stupid. It's not gonna bite ya."

"I don't care, I'm not touchin' it."

"Look, I can't do this on my own. If ya don't lift it up a can't do the rest."

"Hang on a minute…" Po disappeared into the kitchen. He returned a moment later holding a pair of bright yellow rubber gloves.

"Right, but I am only gonna lift it up, nothin' more."

"Right, right, come on."

They entered the room again. Jumpy hadn't moved. Red nodded to Po who had donned the gloves. He grimaced at Red and reached across to Jumpy. He took his penis between his first finger and thumb, crumpling up his face again in disgust. Red had positioned himself underneath Po's arm. In his hand he had a large bar of Bourneville Dark Chocolate. He separated the chocolate squares and began placing them under Jumpy's testicles and between his legs. Red then motioned to Po to let go and move back. He then carefully pulled Jumpy's underpants back up and replaced the bedclothes.

When they were both back in the lounge they sat down and, as if on cue, burst out laughing.

"We got away with it," giggled Po.

"Just…I thought he was gonna wake up a couple a times."

After more laughing and talking, both went off to bed.

Next morning, Red was first up and went around quietly waking the others. He started with Anto, who was still on the sofa. He told him what he and Po had done to Jumpy the night before. Anto's face broke into a broad grin. When the other two were similarly awakened and in the lounge, Red explained part two of his plan. The meeting finished, they marched off giggling to Jumpy's room.

"Mornin' Jumpy, get up ya lazy bastard," shouted Red.

"What? Go away," growled Jumpy.

"We all have ta go somewhere. You'd better get up now, we're late."

"Go where, piss off, go away and die, I have a friggin' headache."

"Too bad, my heart bleeds for ya…up!" roared Anto.

"Right, right, gimme me a friggin' minute, will ya?"
Jumpy sat up in the bed and rubbed his eyes.
"Jasus, I'm wrecked."
"Come on Jumpy, get your ass in gear," chipped in Naffy.
Jumpy mumbled something inaudible and began to move. He suddenly stopped and acquired a puzzled look on his face. Pulling back the bedclothes from the wall side of the bed he looked down under them. He stared for a moment and quickly pulled the clothes back up to his chin.
"You guys piss on outta here and lemme get up and dressed," mumbled Jumpy.
"Ya afraid we might see your wee willie, Jumpy?" smirked Po.
"Piss off will ya."
"Ah come on sleepy head, I'll give ya a hand."
Before Jumpy could say no, Red had grabbed the bedclothes and pulled them off the bed onto the floor. As if rehearsed, all four mouths dropped open and produced gasps.
"Jasus Christ Jumpy," said Red quietly.
They all were looking at the vision of Jumpy sitting up in the bed with a large part of the sheet under him and half his underpants covered in an ominous brown stain.
"Jumpy, you dirty bastard," moaned Naffy.
"Could you not have got up and used the toilet?"
"That's disgustin'," said Po, holding his nose.
To say that poor Jumpy was mortified would be a gross understatement. He was close to tears. Red sat down on the edge of the bed and placed his hand on Jumpy's shoulder.
"Jumpy, we're all mates here, so don't be worryin', we won't tell anybody about this…well, not too many anyways."
"Frig me, frig me…" Jumpy kept repeating to himself.
"Now Jumpy, I wouldn't normally touch ya with Po's dick, never mind my own. But in the state you're in right now you've some nerve even askin'!"
This brought howls of laughter from everyone. Red looked down at the bed clothes where Jumpy was sitting and screwed up his face.

"Christ Jumpy, that looks disgustin', it really does…" He reached into the brown mess under Jumpy's thighs and ran his fingers through it, bringing them up in front of his face.

"Yeah, no doubt about it, that's disgustin', but…" he placed both fingers into his mouth and began sucking to the gasps of all there, even Jumpy.

"…but, I must admit, it doesn't taste too bad!" For a moment Red thought Jumpy's eyes were going to pop out of his head. Then the surprised, puzzled, expression on Jumpy's face slowly began to change as the realization took hold that he'd been had and big time!

As Red opened his front door that night he stopped and smiled. 'Revenge can be very sweet.'

End

The Big Pike

"So, all I have ta do is tell the boys ya saw the big pike at the weir?" asked Red Morgan.

"That's it, great idea huh?" replied Jammy McAteer.

"If it works, it'll be brilliant," laughed Red.

"Right, see ya at half two then Red."

"Yo."

"Yo."

"Shit, this'll be worth seein' wouldn't miss it for the world," whispered Po Hillen as he and Red walked along the canal with seven other members of the gang. Red elbowed Po giving him a look that said, 'Keep your voice down, dickhead'. Earlier Red had been telling the boys about the enormous pike spotted by Jammy in the Clanrye River. Every one of them was eager to go and see if they too could spot this great fish. Red let Po in on the plan, pointed a finger in his face and reminded Po that he was now in debt…big time!

Just after two o'clock the gang set out from Uncle Luigi's. It took fifteen minutes for them to reach Sugar Island Bridge where they turned right along the path of the canal. Five minutes later they came to a single eighteen inch drainage pipe that ran across the canal at water level. Red crossed first. He had walked this pipe many times before and made it look easy. Po was next and made hard work of it.

"Po will ya hurry up for Christ's sake," shouted Red.

His encouragement was echoed by the rest of the boys who were lined up behind Po.

"Shut up, will ya, I'm doin' the best I can."

A few moments later Po reached Red and the rest of the lads followed amid lots of taunting and teasing. The Clanrye River ran parallel to the Newry Canal. They were separated by a one hundred and fifty yard bank. Jammy was already there with his German Shepherd, Prince. He was a big dog weighing over one hundred and thirty pounds, and that was before dinner! After the usual irreverent greetings, Jammy started telling the boys about the big pike he saw that morning in the pool on the other side of the weir.

"I'm tellin' ya, it must have been well over three foot long."

"Where was it exactly?" asked Blackie Havern.

"Over there in the wee pool," answered Jammy pointing.

"Well let's go over and see if it's still there then," piped in Naffy McKay.

"Ok, Red, hold on ta Prince, will ya?" said Jammy, winking at Red.

A four foot wall ran all the way across and twelve inches under the fast flowing river. The wall was eight inches wide and quite slippery. On one side, the water was about four foot deep; on the other it rushed down a thirty yard concrete slope topped with cobblestones. It was a tricky task to traverse in bare feet.

Jammy, already barefoot, was across the wall quickly. When all the socks and shoes had been removed the gang started their slow careful journey across the wall. Red and Po took enough time removing their shoes to ensure they crossed last. Red was still holding onto the alert Prince's collar. Jammy waited until all the boys were on the wall to raise his arm in the air, which was the signal to Red.

"Here Prince, come on boy," yelled Jammy at the top of his voice.

Prince needed no further encouragement and took off in the direction of Jammy. Nothing or no one was going to stop him! With his great body weight, power and balance Prince made short work of the first five feet of the wall. It was there that he met his first obstacle, Naffy McKay. Naffy heard Prince splashing behind him in the water and looked around. He realised the inevitability. Red heard him scream.

"Oh shit, no, go back Prince, Prince!"

But alas, Naffy's plea was in vain. Prince brushed past him as if he wasn't there, knocking him aside and off the wall. Naffy sailed down the cobble stoned slope screaming and swearing. Prince took out the line of weir crossers like skittles. In no time they were all on their way down the cobble stones into the swirling white water at the bottom.

Later that day Red and Po were standing outside Uncle Luigi's when Bishop Keenan and Dunno McManus arrived.

"Yo boys, hi, ya look very clean today, did ya have a bath or somethin'?"

"Oh friggin' hilarious Morgan," snapped Bishop.

"Ya know Red, I'm convinced you and that wee prick Hillen had somethin' to do with us gettin' dumped in the water."

"Too right they were, them bastards were the only ones not on the weir, a wee bit of a coincidence huh?" added Dunno McManus.

"Me?" pleaded Red with arms outstretched and in his best innocent voice.

"I can't believe ya would think that about me. Me, who's been your friend for more years than I can remember, me who's stuck by ya through thick and thin, mostly thick."

Dunno and Bishop looked at each other.

"I told ya he was involved," said Dunno.

"Get the bastard," snarled Bishop.

By this time Po and Red were fifty yards away waving their goodbyes and wearing broad, but not so innocent grins.

End

The Dinger

1959

In the late 1950s, there were basically three items that gave children many hours of pleasure on a daily basis. The first was a rope, which the girls used for swings and skipping, singly or in pairs. There were many chanting rhymes for these games which could last for hours. The boys too made swings. The rope would be doubled and tied at one end, then looped through itself and tied to a telephone pole. They would swing around the pole until the rope was completely used up, somewhat like a Maypole, then swing back in the opposite direction.

The second was a ball. For boys the main games were Football, Cricket, Rounders, and Handball. As for the girls, they used them more in games of juggling. Using two balls, sometimes three or more, these games were played against a wall or between two players. Like skipping these games had chanting rhymes. Another game played by the girls was 'Donkey in the Middle'. One, in the middle of a ring of girls tried to touch the ball being thrown from one to the other. If the girl in the middle touched the ball, the person who threw it would replace her.

The third item, most often used by boys, was a bag of glass marbles or 'Marleys' as they were known. There were many types of marbles, the most widely used were the smallest. These were usually clear glass with a twisting design running through the middle. Depending on the colour in the centre, they all had names like, Tiger's Eye, Dragon's Eye and Cat's Eye. Everyone had what was known as a 'Dinger'. This was a favourite or lucky marble, which, in fact was no different from many others, but had been given credit for winning lots of games. A variety of games were played with marbles and perhaps the most popular was Ringers. This had to be played on earth as opposed to footpaths or concrete. A circle was drawn in the dirt and all players placed a marble inside. Three strides were taken out from this circle where a line was drawn. This was known as the 'Butt'. The idea was to hit the marbles inside the circle and try and knock them out. Any marbles knocked out were then claimed by the shooter.

Po's dinger had a green and white twisting design through its centre. He had this dinger for over a month, which, in dinger life was a long time. Red's dinger had a blue and white twisting design through its core, but his was only two weeks old. Po called his Dinger, Lucky Dragon.
"Lucky Dragon will clean up again taday."
"Yeah? I will own it after the first game," teased Red.
"With what? That stupid wee thing? I think it's lopsided."
"Oh so funny, my sides are bursting," smirked Red.

They had arrived in Hyde Market, a steep hill running from Castle Street to Hill Street. In the middle was an area of grass bordered with shrubs and flowers. Down at the flat end where some of the grass had worn away with constant use, five or six of the boys were already engaged in a game of Ringers. Red and Po had to wait until it was over to get their marbles into the circle.

After playing for thirty minutes, Red had won two. Po was doing much better and was up six.
"Can I play?" came a voice from behind Po.
He looked around and saw the pretty face of Betty Sands.
"Well, good question Betty, can ya play?"
"Don't be stupid Po, of course I can, I'm a lot better than you for sure."

Po glanced at Red who was grinning.

"I have no objections, I need some more marbles anyway, they might as well be yours as anyone else's," smiled Po.

An hour later Red and Po were sitting on a wall at the back of Red's house.

"I can't believe it, that bitch took my dinger."

"No, she didn't take it Po, she won it."

"She cheated."

"How?"

"How the frig do I know, she just did."

"I think she's a good player."

"She's not a good player, she's a cheater."

"What ya can't stand is the fact that ya lost your marbles, especially your dinger, ta a wee girl!"

"Shit."

"True."

"No it's not, she put a hex on me so she did."

"Ah, that's what it was then, a hex. I knew it had ta be somethin'. Are ya comin' down ta Uncle Luigi's?"

"No."

"Why, fraid you're gonna get a hard time about losin' all ya marbles to a girl?"

"Piss off."

"I knew it."

"Look, I didn't friggin' lose, I was cheated."

"Ok then, I came out evens. I will give ya six of mine to go back and play Betty again."

"No."

"Afraid?"

"No, I have lost ma dinger sure."

"Ah that's right, so ya can never play marleys ever again."

"Well not until I get another one."

"How can ya get a dinger if ya don't play?"

"Well, I'm not gonna play with that bitch cheat."

"Two days ago ya were tellin' me that Betty was very pretty and had lovely legs. She turns out ta be a good marble player, cleans ya out, takes your dinger and all of a sudden she's ugly, a bitch, a witch and a cheat."

"They're all the same, next thing ya know they'll be wantin' ta play football!"

"Katie Jones plays for Church Street."

"She's different."

"She's a girl."

"Yeah, but she's like one of the lads."

"Jasus Po ya come up with some stupid arguments."

"Anyway, girls shouldn't be allowed ta play boy's games."

"Ya, I'm sure you're right Po, but ya left out somethin', they shouldn't be allowed ta play boys games if they're better than the boys."

"Oh frig off."

End

The Dentist

1960

"No, I'm not goin' and that's that," moaned Po to his best friend Red Morgan as they sat on the steps at the junction of Castle Street and Hyde Market. He was holding his jaw as if in some way by doing so it would ease the pain in his mouth emanating from an angry molar.

"But if ya don't go ya'll be in pain for the rest of the day, the rest of the week, shit, the rest of your life," returned Red seriously.

"The guy's a butcher, a sadist."

"That's a load of crap and ya know it, but, I suppose ya need all the excuses ya can get. The fact is you're just afraid ya'll look bad, a coward like."

"What de ya mean…afraid? I'm not afraid and I'm not a coward. I just don't like dentists, who does?"

"Don't believe it for a minute. He puts a mask over your gob, ya drift off and dream of Mary Fearon and when ya wake up, no more pain, tooth gone."

"Will ya listen ta who's talkin'. Mr. Brave, the hero. I had ta practically drag ya inta the dentist's last time ya had ta go."

"Ach sure I was very young then, I didn't know any better."

"Jasus, so you've grown up in this past six months have ya?"

"This is not the point, its half past three now, ya have ta be there for four o'clock, so come on, sure I'll hold your wee hand and won't let the bad dentist hurt ya."

"He makes ya rinse your mouth out with that pink shit. It makes me sick so it does."

"So don't use it, ask for water or somethin'."

"The smell of the place makes me sick."

"So breathe through your mouth."

"I don't like him."

"So what, ya like the blonde in reception and she likes ya."

"How de ya know that?"

"Sure she couldn't take her eyes of ya the whole time ya were in the waitin' room last time, I was watchin' her."

"You're lyin' through your teeth Morgan."

"Would I lie ta ma bestest friend in the whole world?"

"Yeah."

"That's a very hurtful thing ta say, it could damage me for life ya know, anyway I only ever tell ya small fibs sometimes, but never about blondes."

"No, not goin' ta do it."

"Ach well, I suppose it's yourself will have ta live with the shame, the sniggerin', the pointin' fingers."

"What are ya on about now?"

"Sure ya know ya'll get the name of a coward all over the town. Ya'll never live it down. No girl will ever go out with ya again, ya'll be teased for ever from ex friends who won't want ta be seen with a coward in case people think they are one too and…"

"All right, all right, I'll go. Anythin' ta shut ya up," shouted Po.

"My hero," laughed Red as he put his arm around Po's shoulders.

"Piss off ya fruit."

At four o'clock on the reception clock Red and Po were sitting on uncomfortable wooden chairs flipping through women's magazines.

"Why is it they never have magazines for men in these places? Ya would think it was only women that went ta the dentist."

"Mr. Hillen," came the voice of the blonde behind the counter. "Go right through please."

"Shit," whispered Po.

"My brave wee man."

"Get stuffed."

Thirty minutes later Po appeared in the doorway and motioned to Red. As they descended the stairs Red placed his arm around Po.

"Are ya ok?"

"No," mumbled Po holding a handkerchief to his mouth.

"Is it sore?"

"Not…too…bad," said Po who was having trouble speaking.

When they arrived at Po's house his mom had just arrived also, from work, and had the key in the door.

"Ach my brave wee soldier, are ya all right are ya? Come on in and lay down for a wee while, sure you're very brave altogether."

Po glanced at Red who was wearing a great grin.

"What are ya grinnin' at?"

"My wee brave soldier, now go and rest your wee self. I will call later with some flowers."

Po was about to give Red a suitable reply when he remembered his mom was still standing beside them.

"Yeah, I'll see ya later Morgan, ya can bet on it."

"Here ya are Red," said Po's mom handing some money to Red.

Po looked at his mom puzzled.

"What's that for?"

"I promised your friend Red I would give him the money for the pictures if he went with you ta the dentists, and isn't he a true friend?" said Mrs. Hillen as she went into the house.

"Ya…ya dirty rotten, stinkin', low down, snake in the grass, lyin' cheatin' fruit."

"Ah Po, now don't be like that, sure I would have went with ya anyway so I would."

"All that shit ya gave me was just ta get me ta go so ya would get the money for the pictures, ya low down bastard snake."

"Ya remember the wee blonde behind the counter?"

"What about her?"

"Didn't I only get ya a date with her for the Parochial Hall on Saturday night."

"Ya did not."

"I did."

"You're lyin'."

"I swear, honest ta God. She is goin' ta meet ya Saturday at nine thirty outside the Parochial."

"Jasus."

"Ya a happy wee toothless person now?"

"Yeah, I suppose."

"See ya later at Luigi's."

"Yeah, see ya later."

As Red walked up North Street he was thinking of the afternoons events.

'Now I have to find a way ta get that wee blonde ta meet Po on Saturday. Jasus, its hard work being a best friend so it is.'

End

Trees are for Monkeys

1960

Red's house, like all the houses on Castle Street, had a marvellous back garden. Not just because they were big, but most had access to old, long abandoned buildings. At the bottom of Red's garden was an old bakery known as Willis's. These areas were a haven in which the kids played; a ready made playground for every conceivable game.

Today in Red's back garden, Dunno McManus and Jumpy Jones were with Po and Red, messing around and doing nothing in particular.
"That's some size tree," said Dunno looking up at the great oak tree at the bottom of the garden in front of the old bakery.
"How tall do ya think it is?"
"Don't know, but it's almost twice the size of Willis's, and that's two stories high," answered Red.
"Did anyone ever climb it?" asked Jumpy.
"Not all the way ta the top. I was half way up a few times."
"It's not all that high," said Po also looking up at the tree.
"Are you nuts, it's the biggest tree I've seen for sure," said Dunno.
"Nobody could climb that tree," suggested Jumpy.
"And why not?" asked Po turning to look at him.
"Po, look at it, it's enormous for Christ's sake."

"So?"

"So, it's just too big ta climb all the way up. I'll bet there's snow on the top."

"Your head's a Marley Jumpy, I could climb it, no bother."

"In your dreams," added Dunno.

"Po, don't even think about it," said Red. "It's too high and thin at the top in the first place, and in the second place it's too high in the first place."

"I'm gonna climb it," stated Po taking off his jacket.

"Po, I'm serious now, I would give this a miss if I were you," said Red in earnest.

"Don't be a wee girl Red; I can climb it. If I thought I couldn't I wouldn't even try."

"Ok, it's your funeral."

Ten minutes later Po had managed to make it almost twenty feet up the tree. He waved down at his watching audience.

"Will he get all the way ta the top?" Jumpy asked no one in particular.

"Knowing Po, he will," said Red.

"Rather him than me," murmured Dunno. "I get dizzy standin' on a chair."

"How ya doin' Po?" shouted Red through cupped hands.

"It's thinnin' out now. The branches are smaller, ya know. It's a lot harder the nearer I get ta the top," came the distant reply.

Po was now three quarters of the way up the tree. The three boys had to move back almost twenty feet to see him.

"The wee bugger's gonna make it ya know," stated Jumpy.

Red heard Po's voice call him.

"Red?"

"What?"

"Red?"

"I can hear ya."

"I'm stuck."

"You're stuck?"

"I'm friggin' stuck for Christ's sake."

"Are ya caught on somethin'?"

"No."

"How de ya mean, you're stuck?"

"I can't move, I just can't move."

"He's looked down and froze I'll bet," said Jumpy.

"Try ta move down slowly Po," shouted Red.

"I can't. I can't."

"Ya have ta try Po," encouraged Red.

"I can't move. The branch is swayin' Red. I think it's gonna break."

Red heard panic in Po's voice.

"Ok. Po, just hold on tight and we'll get help. Hold on tight. Do ya hear?"

"Yeah."

"Jumpy, run as fast as ya can and get my dad. Tell him what's happenin', right?"

"I'm gone."

A short time later Red's dad and some of the neighbours arrived on the scene. They had a ladder, but even when extended it came nowhere near to where Po was on the tree.

"Red, go to Bradley's shop and tell Lilly to ring the Fire Brigade," said Red's dad.

Almost twenty minutes later two firemen arrived.

"We'll need the engine extension for this," stated the one in the white hat looking up at the tree.

"How will we get it here? This is gonna be a problem."

The fireman with the white hat spoke to Red's dad.

"Is there another entrance from Hill Street?"

Well there's Boyle's Shop, they have a gate, but I'm not sure if the fire engine will get in."

"Ok, we'll try it. Tom, take the appliance to Hill Street. I'll go through this way and have a look."

"Are you his mate?" the fireman asked Red.

"Yes."

"Ok, now keep talkin' ta him. Reassure him. Tell him we'll get him down very soon, ok?"

"Ok."

Red kept a running conversation with Po. In what seemed a very short span of time the fire crew had backed the engine through Boyle's side gate. They were able to get close enough to use the extension ladder and finally, manoeuvred it near enough to get hold of Po.

Two hours later Red and Po were sitting in Uncle Luigi's drinking coffee.

"Well now," said Red, his first words since their arrival.

"Don't."

"Don't what?"

"Don't start giving me a hard time, I'm not in the mood."

"Would I do that? I was only gonna say the coffee was nice."

"Yeah, right, sure ya were."

"Ach well, sure wasn't it a grand experience altogether?"

"No, it wasn't."

"Shit, I enjoyed it for sure. A lot better than playin' some stupid game ta pass the time."

"I have ta go home yet and tell my parents what happened. I'd be better off if I'd fallen out of that friggin' tree."

Red laughed.

"What lesson have we learned today Mr. Hillen?"

"What?"

"Trees are for monkeys! What did we learn?"

"Friggin' trees are for friggin' monkeys, ok?"

"Ya know, I think ya got it."

"Red?"

"Yeah?"

"You'll never let me forget this, will ya?"

"No."

"If I were ta take ya to the pictures this Saturday?"

"No."

"If I were ta give you them football cards ya like?"

"No."

"How about if I put a word in for ya with your one Betty Hanna?"

"Hmmm."

"I'll tell her you're great."

"At least ya won't be lyin'. "

"Go on, will ya?"

"I'll think about it."

"Bastard."

"Trees are for monkeys!" said Red, shaking his finger at Po.

End

The Yacht

1960

The referee gave three short shrill blows on his whistle to indicate the end of the match. Po and Red were already hugging each other on the floor of the Warrenpoint Town Hall. It was the end of the indoor 'Five a Side' Final and Red and Po's team, West End United, had won 3 – 2.

Supporters were streaming onto the floor to congratulate the team. Red and Po and the other players were now surrounded. Back slaps, handshakes, hair rubs, hoisting onto shoulders, jerseys being swung in the air, even in some cases, kissing, were in abundance. West End were the underdogs in the tournament which made the victory even sweeter for both players and spectators.

When they eventually got back to the dressing rooms clutching the large silver Warrenpoint Festival Five-a-Side Cup, the hugging started all over again. Each player wore a gold medal around his neck. They were dancing and screaming with delight. Quite simply, the mood was jubilant.

Some two hours later, the team had been fed and watered close to bursting. Red and Po were walking along the sea front reliving the night's events blow by blow.

"How much have ya?" asked Po.

"About five bob, why?"

"I've ten, let's get some booze!"

"Sounds like an idea to me."

Ten minutes later they were sitting on the beach beside the pier drinking John Powers Irish Whiskey from the bottle.

"What time is the last bus did you say Po?"

"Half-eleven."

"For shit sake Po, it's ten past twelve!"

"Couldn't be."

"It is. Now what'll we do?"

"If ya didn't talk so much we'd be home now."

Red slapped him on the back of the head and they both laughed.

"Ok, right, let's get our heads together and sort this problem," said Red.

"We need ta find a way home. Hitchin' a lift will be a waste of time. The road will be full of birds headin' home from the dances. Nobody will stop for us, that's for sure," Red continued.

"Yeah, you're right. We could sleep here if we had some blankets, its warm enough."

"Might be warm enough now, but it'll get cold later."

"I could do with a nice cosy bed about now too," moaned Po.

"Me too."

They both sat silently for a few moments. Suddenly Po sat upright.

"A nice bed did ya say?"

"Yeah, why?"

"Sure amin't I lookin' at one?"

"What?"

"Sure I'm only a genius."

"Po, gimme that bottle, you've had too much."

Po stood up and went behind Red. He took his head between his hands and pointed Red's face in the direction of the pier.

"See?"

"See what?"

"Beds."

"Beds? What the frig are you on about?"

"There dopey."

"There's nothin' there but boats ya twit."

"Jasus, you're smart."

"Wait a minute…" Red stood up.

"Are you sayin' we should go out there ta the boats and…"

"Why the hell not? I got it all figured. Look, it's only about a hundred yards, right? We'll hide our clothes under the bridge there and swim out."

"That's all very well but…"

"There's a bus at six-thirty in the mornin', we'll get that. We can get inta one of them boats, they have beds ya know, and sleep till about six…whaddya think?"

Red thought about it for a moment, "We'll do it, let's go."

A few minutes later they were both naked, had hidden their clothes under the walkway, and were toe dipping the not so warm Carlingford Lough water. It took them about five minutes to reach the boat they had selected. It was called 'Greencastle Queen'. They clambered on board and eventually found a window slightly open. A few moments later they were inside and had found the bunks. In ten minutes they were both fast asleep.

Red opened his eyes and tried to remember where he was. He could hear the water lapping outside, it was daylight. Wrapping a sheet around himself he crossed the small cabin to where Po was still sleeping.

"Hi, Po, wakeup."

"What time is it?"

"Don't know, but we'd better get outta here."

"Right, right, lemme get my head together."

Red went up on deck while Po was going through his morning routine of stretching, yawning, scratching and moaning. Moments later Red came bolting into the cabin. His face was now well flushed and he was breathing hard.

"We are in shit, big time."

Po looked up at him, still not fully awake.

"What?"

"Go up on deck."

"What are ya talkin' about?"

"Go!"

Po wrapped a sheet around himself and clambered up the steep steps. The sun was warm on his face. He closed his eyes for a moment of enjoyment. The sound of children screaming and laughing made him open them quickly. Po looked toward the shoreline. The beach was full of people…hundreds of them.

He felt Red squeeze up beside him.

"I just found a clock, it's friggin' half past eleven!"

"Oh Christ, what'll we do?"

Red disappeared back down the steps. Over his shoulder Po heard him say something about clothes. Po followed him.

"Look around and see if ya can find any clothes," muttered Red.

After fifteen minutes they gave up. No clothes were to be found on the boat.

"What'll we do now Red?" asked Po worriedly.

"Well, we can't stay here, that's for sure. The people who own this boat could be on their way here right now."

"Shit."

"We'll have ta make a run for it, swim ashore, hope our clothes are still there and get the hell home."

"We can't do that, don't be stupid, the beach is full of women, and they're where our clothes are hidden too."

"Look Po, ask yourself, have we a friggin' choice?"

"Suppose not."

"You suppose right, come on."

Both slipped into the cool waters and swam for the shoreline. When they reached a depth where they could stand on the bottom, both stopped to get a breather and get ready to make their run for the walkway.

"Red…Po?"

They swapped glances when they heard their names called by a loud female voice. Looking toward the beach Red spotted the waving arms of Mrs. McKnight and her three kids.

"Shit no," whispered Po who had just spotted her.

"What'll we do?"

"Wave."

"What?"

"Wave for Christ's sake."

Both were now waving, but the smiles on their faces were hard to maintain.

"We've gotta go for it Po."

"I know, I know, don't remind me."

They started swimming again, and were now close to the wall of the pier. The water was now only inches deep.

"We'll have ta make a run for it, are ya right?"

"I hate this, I hate it."

"Right…go!"

They were now running through the last few feet of water. In minutes they were on the beach, hands covering what they considered the most important parts of their bodies. They made about ten yards when they heard the voice of Mrs. McKnight again.

"Hi Po…nice bum."

They heard the laughter spread through the sunbathers. Some were sitting up, shading their eyes to get a better view. One woman even had the cheek to look through a pair of binoculars! The laughter soon broke into applause. Red and Po's faces took on the appearance of bad sunburn.

With great relief, the boys reached the spot where they had left their clothes and found them still there. Never before had they dressed so quickly. Within minutes they were running at top speed as far away from Mrs. McKnight as their legs would take them.

Later that day Po and Red were sitting in Uncle Luigi's relating the story to a couple of the gang.

"It was all that wee frigger's idea, I should a known better," said Red pointing a finger into Po's face.

"No one forced ya ta agree."

Just then a group of women entered the café with prams and trailing children. One stopped at the boys snug.

"Well, well, if it isn't the Newry Streakers," said Mrs. Connelly, who lived near Red on Castle Street. Po and Red got the sunburned look again and started inspecting their hands, while the rest of the lads broke into laughter. Both made a hasty exit and ran as fast as they could toward home. When they had reached the top of Mill Street they stopped for a breather.

"That's it, ruined, finished for all time. I'll have to move out of Newry, that's all there is to it," panted Po with his hands on his knees trying to catch his breath. Red was leaning against a wall. He slid down to the footpath and suddenly began to laugh.

"What's so friggin' funny?"

"You."

"What about me?"

"Well at least ya came out of it with some admirers."

"What are ya talkin' about?"

Between laughs Red continued.

"Well, now ya'll be known as Po, 'nice bum' Hillen."

"Oh very, very funny ya bastard," snarled Po as he began slapping Red about the head.

Red was on his feet quickly and over his shoulder he quipped, "Well, ya do have a nice bum Po, well shaped, ya know, sort of appealing."

"Piss off ya queer…ya fruit…ya no good bastard…"

Red felt a thump between his shoulders as he ran up Castle Street. Looking back he saw Po's shoe on the footpath and ducked just in time to miss the second one.

The day of the 'Five a Side' Cup Final will long be remembered, for some the triumph of the great win and for others the sight of two pink bums on Warrenpoint beach.

End

Swimming with the Fishes

1960

Po and Red were sitting on the hard floor in the back of the light blue Volkswagen Pick-up truck as it made its way south along the narrow twisting and bumpy Omeath Road. They were on their way to Narrow Water with Red's Uncle Pajoe Morgan and the owner of the van, Jackie McCain. Narrow Water was just over half way to Omeath, a small seaside village over the border in County Louth. Both Red and Po loved these trips. Spending a Sunday conger fishing was as good as it gets.

The van swung left onto a narrow lane and soon came to a lurching halt. They had arrived. It was Red and Po's job to get the fishing lines and equipment out of the van while Pajoe and Jackie examined the area. After pacing the shoreline and having much debate on the position of the sun and the tide, their fishing spots were chosen.

The lines were made of whip cord and were approximately one hundred and fifty yards long. The large hooks were about four inches long and curled into a barbed point. During the week it had been Red and Po's job to make the weights. These consisted of empty boot polish tins filled with melted lead and allowed to set. The lead was then extracted and a hole punched through to which the line was tied. They were ready…well…almost. The lines had to be plaited. They were tied to a hook specially put into the wall in Red's back yard and plaited for eighteen inches much the same way women plait their hair. The hook would be placed on the loop at the front of the plait and the weight near the end.

Everything was ready; they all took their selected spots and the fishing began in earnest. The hooks were placed inside herrings, which were the conger's favourite snack. The four fishermen were situated about ten yards apart. With this type of fishing plenty of space is needed. No fishing rods are used, so the cast entailed the hook and weight being swung above the head in a circular motion and released. The weight carries the line well out into the water where it sinks to the bottom. The line is then slowly drawn back toward the shore. Conger eels, sometimes as long as five feet, swim and feed on the bottom and take the bait as it is pulled along.

An hour had passed and Jackie was the only one who had any luck. He'd netted two fairly big eels. The rest of them only had the odd nibble. Po was getting bored and decided to move further up the beach to the pier. He shouted to Red and pointed to where he was going. Red waved and started to move nearer the pier himself. The pier rose some ten feet above the water and was a lucky spot for Po who had netted many fish from there in the past. It was also more comfortable because after the line was cast, one could sit on the edge and slowly draw it in, whereas on the beach, standing was the only option.

Another fifteen minutes passed and Red netted a small eel. He was holding it in the air waving at Po who remained the only one who had yet to catch anything. Suddenly Po's line went taught. He'd got one at last. Po yelled to Red and pointed. The way the line was moving, Red knew it was a big one. Po was frantically beckoning Red to help him. After tying his line to a large stone, Red raced towards the pier. He was watching Po's line as it suddenly slackened. The fish had turned and was moving toward the pier. Po kept taking in slack as quickly as he could.

"It's a friggin' monster," Po shouted to Red who was now only a few feet away.

"Hurry up for Christ's sake!"

Red had almost reached Po when the fish turned again and took off in the opposite direction. He saw Po's arms straighten in front of him before he began sailing through the air off the edge of the pier. There was a great splash as Po hit the water. Red ran back down the pier's slope to the water level on the beach in time to greet a distraught Po wading ashore. Pajoe and Jackie had now joined the boys.

"Shitface, bastard, whore," Po was mumbling over and over again to no one in particular.

Pajoe, wearing a broad grin looked at Red.

"What's he sayin'?"

"Something about shit I think," piped in Jackie.

"That's what I thought I heard," said Pajoe.

"Did ya want a toilet Po?"

"Don't start, just don't start you lot of bastards."

"Did ya go for a wee swim son?" said Jackie with a straight face.

"That bastard caught me off balance," spat Po taking off his sodden jacket.

"What bastard?" asked Red seriously.

"What bastard do ya think for Christ's sake, the friggin' conger."

"Conger? What conger?" said Red turning towards Pajoe.

"What's he sayin' Red? He saw a conger?"

"He says he jumped in after a conger," answered Red.

"I didn't say that a'tall ya bastard, a giant enormous conger pulled me off the friggin' pier, you saw it."

It was now Jackie's turn to add his penny's worth.

"Look, Po. Maybe I should a mentioned this to ya before, but we use these lines here to catch the congers, ya see. Sure if we were to jump in and try to catch them by hand, we'd get frig all don't ya know…them whores can swim at some speed."

"Will ya all piss off, I'm friggin' soaked, my watch is friggin' ruined, and I've lost a bastard shoe and all you lot can do is take the piss."
Jackie looked at Red.
"I thought it was a shit he wanted, it's a piss now I heard him say."
"Can ya believe that, try ta give someone a wee bit of advice and all ya get is the worst word in his mouth."
"Ach sure it's a disgrace, these young fellas nowadays have no respect a'tall."
"Ya know, I knew a fella one time…"
"Red, I'm warning ya, ya come out with one more smartarse remark and I'll split ya with one of these stones."

All three walked off down the beach to their respective lines chatting as they went.
"No respect."
"Disgraceful."
"It's the way they're reared ya know."
"Bad schoolin' I put it down ta."
"Hangin's too good for these young ones; a good slap across the face is what they need!"

All the way home Po sat in his usual place on the floor of the truck with an old dog blanket wrapped around him and his fingers in his ears. He thought to himself, 'The word 'mate' should be taken out of the friggin' dictionary. There's no such friggin' thing.'

End

Red the Hero

1960

Red and Po were strolling along the lane at the back of High Street houses discussing the football practice that had just finished.

"What was that?" asked Red.

"What?"

"Shush a minute."

They listened for a moment, then Po heard it too.

"Help, somebody, help."

It was a female voice.

Without a word, both ran in the direction from which the voice seemed to be coming. They reached an open back gate to one of the houses and raced through. Tightly squeezed into the corner between the house and garden wall was Collette Cummings.

Collette was a young lady who Red had been trying to date. Having just moved back to Newry from England, she was of great interest to all the young men of the town; maybe the fact that she was tall and quite beautiful had something to do with it, but so far, Red's efforts had proved fruitless.

Sitting in front of Collette was an enormous Rottweiler, showing his large and ferocious looking teeth.

"Please get it away, it's goin' ta bite me," whimpered Collette.

"Ok Collette, just stay calm now. Don't move, just stay perfectly still." Red started moving in a circular motion towards Collette.

"Po, move out slowly and check ta make sure McDonald's gate is open."

Po moved backwards out of the yard. Red was now almost between the dog and Collette.

"Collette, start towards the back door."

"Ok," replied Collette very softly, almost in a whisper.

Red was now directly between the dog and Collette. He started talking to the dog softly.

"Good boy, stay, stay," he was looking intently into the dog's eyes. The Rottweiler was still showing his teeth.

"Collette, keep moving towards the back door."

She moved slowly sideways along the gable wall of the house in the direction of the back door which was about ten feet away. Red continued to talk to the dog softly and had begun moving towards him. He heard the back door open for a few seconds and close. Knowing she was now in the safety of the house, he slowly reached out and started patting the dog's head gently with his left hand. With the other hand he took hold of his collar, still talking softly to him. Red was aware that Collette was watching him from the kitchen window and this made him a little nervous. He got a good grip on the collar and began turning the dog towards the gate. The dog accepted this and walked with him. When outside the gate, Red reached back and pulled it closed.

Po was standing about twenty feet away, just past McDonald's. Red walked quickly now until he reached the open gate. He turned into the yard.

"Red, be careful now," he heard Po's shaky voice.

Red turned and looked at Po with a broad grin across his face. He was still holding the Rottweiler's collar. Kneeling down beside the seemingly calm and happy dog, he began to cuddle him. The dog in return started licking Red's face and furiously wagging his back end.

Eventually Red closed the gate, saying goodbye, and marched off towards Po still wearing a broad grin.

"Jasus Red, you're somethin' else, ya got nerves of friggin' steel."

"Ya think so? What makes ya say that?"

"Handlin' the dog like that, he could a ripped ya ta pieces, did ya see his teeth? Holy Jasus, the size of him too," Po blew his cheeks out. "A tell ya, I would not for love nor money have gone anywhere near him!"

Red began laughing and had to stop and lean against a wall.

"What the hell are ya laughin' at?"

"Po, it's like this ya see. That ferocious big dog is called Jake. He's owned by the McDonalds. I've known him since he was a pup."

"But he was showin' his teeth, he was gonna attack."

"No way, he does that all the time. He copied that from people who smiled when they greeted him when he was a pup. He's smilin'. As for killin' ya, the only way Jake would kill ya would be ta lick ya ta death."

"Holy Shit."

"Now ya have it."

"So all that back there…?" Po was pointing back toward Collette's house.

"Yep."

"You sneaky bastard."

"All compliments gratefully received."

"Now she thinks you're a friggin' big hero who risked his life ta save her?"

"Yep, that would be me all right."

"You'll have no bother gettin' out with her now, will ya?"

"Looks that way," smiled Red.

"You are one, sneaky, jammy bastard Morgan."

"Right ya are. But hey, don't forget, clever bastard too."

End

Paper Money

1960

Po looked at his watch, lifted a crushed cardboard shoe box and threw it at Red who was working ten feet away. They were in the Newry Council's local refuse dump collecting paper and cardboard and packing it into large bales. The local 'Rag Store' bought paper at one shilling a stone (14lbs). It was a warm summer Saturday afternoon and the gang had been working from eleven o'clock that morning. All the usual faces were there, Red Morgan, Po Hillen, Kitter Murray, Jammy McAteer and Shifty McShane

"Hi, it's almost three o'clock," shouted Po.

"So?"

"The Rag Store closes at five today."

"Shit, forgot about that, we'd better get Humpy John or we'll miss him."

"I'll go."

"Ok, don't be all day."

Po just answered with two fingers and went off toward the main Armagh Road.

So far they had collected three large bales which were well tied and ready to go. Each one weighed an estimated five stone. Humpy John lived about half a mile away and had a donkey and cart. He'd made arrangements with the gang earlier and for a fee of two shillings, he would transport the day's pickings to Maggie Smith's Rag Store.

Twenty minutes later Po's voice made Red look in the direction of the main gate. He was standing on the back of Humpy John's cart pretending he had a rifle and was shooting everything in sight. Some of the lad's were returning fire and Po took a hit to the chest, which he grabbed dramatically and fell backwards into the cart.

"He's not the full shillin' ya know," laughed Kitter Murray.

"Is that supposed to be news?" quipped Red.

"He was born nuts."

Under the instruction of Humpy John, the donkey and cart came to a halt beside the three bales of paper.

"Whoa there Lucy, whoa."

The three bales were pushed and pulled up the makeshift ramp and into the cart which complained by creaking under the weight. The procession of Lucy, pulling the cart, Humpy John walking alongside her and the boys, two on each side and one at the back, moved onto the Armagh Road. This downhill part of the one mile journey to the Rag Store was the easiest. Then they turned right onto Catherine Street which was 'L' shaped; the first half being a steep hill. Lucy, urged on by Humpy John, was pulling hard, and her five helpers were now at the back of the cart pushing as hard as they could. Humpy John was holding two wedge shaped pieces of wood which every few yards he would push under the wheels to halt the proceedings and give Lucy a rest.

They reached halfway up the incline and were making good progress; but this time, when the wedges were removed, the bales slipped backward in the cart. Spotting a potential disaster, Humpy John quickly got the wedges back behind the wheels. This stopped the cart from going backward, but with the weight now shifted, the cart tilted and in a matter of seconds Lucy was airborne! Judging from her reaction she was not a happy donkey. She started 'hee hawing' loudly with her legs running wildly but getting nowhere. Humpy John gave instructions for everyone to get into the front of the cart. The boys complied with the exception of Po who lost his footing and landed on his backside on the road much to the delight of everyone who cheered and applauded.

Eventually the cart levelled out and Lucy got back to terra firma. They managed, with much moaning and groaning, to move the bales forward again and the procession was ready to continue. By this time most of the residents of Catherine Street had come to their front doors to watch the show and were applauding and cheering the efforts to right the cart. For them, the sight of a donkey three feet off the ground, complaining loudly, on a Saturday afternoon was, if not unusual, definitely entertaining.

Fifteen minutes later Lucy, who had now calmed down, was stopped at Maggie Smith's Rag Store. When the bales were weighed, the total earnings, less Humpy John's expenses, came to two shillings and nine pence each. Enough to go to the Cinema get some crisps and ice cream, five Woodbine, and some chips on the way home. A good day's earnings by all accounts.

"Jasus, my arse is sore," complained Po on the walk home.
"If ya weren't so friggin' awkward ya wouldn't have landed on it in the first place," pointed out Jammy McAteer. A murmur of agreement followed.
"There was friggin' grease on the friggin' wheel," complained Po.
"There's grease in your friggin' head," quipped Red.
"Aye, go on, have a good laugh ya bastards. Like none of ya ever fell before," moaned Po.
"Well not in front of thirty people on Catherine Street, and with that wee one ya fancy, what's her name?" Red turned to Kitter Murray for help.
"Mavis O'Hanlon."
"That's the one."
"She wasn't there?" Po said to Red almost pleadingly.
"She was, at her mate's house, I saw her."
"You're a lyin' bastard Morgan."
"Kitter……am I lyin'?"

"No, she was there all right, I seen her."

"Yis are all lyin' friggin' bastards."

Ten minutes later the gang had split up and Po and Red were walking up Mill Street.

"Red, tell the truth now, was Mavis O'Hanlon there?"

"Yep."

"She wasn't."

"She was."

Po put his face in his hands and moaned.

"I'm skundered, come on Red, tell me she wasn't there."

"She wasn't there."

"I knew it."

"Knew what?"

"She wasn't there."

"She was."

"You just said she wasn't!"

"That's because ya asked me ta tell ya that."

"You're a total bastard Morgan."

"I know," smiled Red.

"She wasn't there."

"She was."

"She wasn't."

"She was."

This lasted all the way home. Some day's are good, some not so good. For Po, this was a not so good day!

End

The High Mass Incident

1960

It took a lot of shouting, arguing, threats, blackmail, and finally bribes, but eventually, both Red Morgan and Po Hillen's families got them to attend Altar Boy classes two days a week, after school. At the conclusion of the six week course, ten of the boys who took the class were examined, and passed by the Parish Priest Father Tom O'Malley.

Red and Po's parents were delighted and when the news broke, generous amounts of spending money were laid upon the boys. Perhaps somewhere in the hidden depths of the parent's minds they saw the tender beginnings of a vocation to the priesthood. It is sometimes marvellous to see how far from reality some parents allow their minds to wander.

Both Po and Red had their first few Masses behind them and were becoming quite proficient at the job. They had agreed however, that this was, in no way, going to be a permanent thing; well, that was at the beginning. Things soon changed when they got to serve at weddings and special Masses. They were amazed and delighted at the number of tips they acquired.

Some six months down the road, our two 'angels' were now senior Altar Boys. Then came the fateful day when they were both serving at High Mass in Newry Cathedral. Po was very nervous about this Mass. He had served at High Masses before, but this time he was put in charge of the Thurible, or incense burner. He had of course been trained in its use but never before used it during Mass.

There were four Altar Boys serving at this evening Mass. They were lined up in their white surpluses and scarlet cassocks waiting to lead His Grace, Bishop Downey, out of the vestry and onto the main altar. Red and Po were at the front because the two other Altar Boys were juniors. This evening, Red would be in charge of the Mass Bells and Po the incense. Red glanced at Po.
"What's wrong with ya? You're still nervous about the incense aren't ya?"
"Nervous? I've pissed four times in this past ten minutes."
"I'll be beside ya for sure. If ya forget anythin' just nudge me, though, I'll probably be remindin' his nibs where he is in the Mass."
Bishop Downey was in his late seventies and to say he was forgetful would be an understatement.

"Right gentlemen, let's not keep the Lord waiting," came the voice of Bishop Downey who had just arrived behind them. Red was holding the bells in his right hand and he rang them three times. This was to inform the congregation that the Mass was about to start and that they should stand. The small group made their way from the sacristy onto the main altar, took their places and the Mass began.

Red was keeping an eye on Po who seemed to be getting more and more nervous as the time approached for him to begin the burning of the incense. The charcoal in the burner was down to its red hot ember state and ready for the incense to be spooned onto it. When the time arrived, Po pulled the middle chain which lifted the lid, incense cup and spoon. The Bishop approached, took a spoonful of incense and sprinkled it on the burning embers. Po released the chain and the sweet smell of incense began to fill the church. Po did everything by the book. He held the Thurible at chest height and swung it forwards and backwards towards the Tabernacle. 'So far so good,' thought Red. He glanced at Po who winked. He was over the worst now and his confidence had returned.

The Bishop approached Po for the second time in the Mass and repeated the sprinkling of the incense on the charcoal. Po continued to do his job with great proficiency, but something went un-noticed the second time the Bishop finished sprinkling the incense. He placed the spoon back, not in the cup with the incense, but on top of the charcoal. Po hadn't noticed this and continued as normal.

Then came the third and final time the Bishop would sprinkle the incense. Po opened the lid to allow the Bishop access only this time, when replacing the spoon, his attention wandered and he placed the now red hot spoon on top of Po's hand. The hushed silence in the Cathedral was broken by one single word.
"Shit!"
Red glanced at Po in disbelief. A shockwave spread among the congregation, but within seconds, the startled silence was broken by the sound of stifled laughter. The Bishop carried on as if nothing had happened and finished the Mass.

When the procession returned to the sacristy a stern faced Father O'Malley was waiting. He pointed to Po, then to a small storeroom. Without a word Po entered the room with Father O'Malley at his heels.

Red helped the Bishop out of his robes and decided to see how the land lay.
"Poor Po," said Red almost apologetically.
"What?"
"I said, 'Poor Po' Your Grace?"
"Who?" The Bishop's face was even more wrinkled than usual in the effort to hear what Red was saying.
"Po!"
"Yes, yes. What did he mean? I didn't hear him right. Did he say something about having a fit?"

"No, he's all right now, Your Grace."

"Ah, good, good. Tell him I will pray for him, good."

Red removed his cassock and surplus and left the Cathedral. He had been waiting for Po almost fifteen minutes when he saw him leaving by the side door.

"Any fags?" asked Po as if nothing had happened.

"No bruises, cuts, broken bones? Did Father Tom die in there or what?"

Po laughed.

"He looked very stern when we went in. Then he said he understood what happened."

"…and?"

"He was strugglin' to keep a straight face, then he gave up the struggle and we both laughed for a few minutes. He was almost cryin'," laughed Po.

"He said if it had been him, he most likely would've said somethin' far worse."

"Jasus, you're a jammy bugger. Ya got off lucky…almost."

Po stopped and took Red by the arm.

"Whaddya mean…almost?"

"Well, the easy bit is ya'll get slagged somethin' awful for the next few weeks, maybe months. Think about the boys in Uncle Luigi's and at school?"

"Frig em, I don't care."

They walked on for a little, Po suddenly stopped again.

"Hey, ya said that was the easy bit, so what'll the hard bit be then?"

"Po, think about it ya ejit. Your mom and dad were at that Mass. Ya still have ta go home tonight don't ya?"

Po looked up at the sky.

"Shit!"

End

The Wake

1960

"Now you make sure you call in to McCall's and pay your respects," Red Morgan's grandmother shouted after him as he left his house in Castle Street.

"I will, I will," Red mumbled over his shoulder.

He walked down towards Hill Street and in a few minutes arrived at Uncle Luigi's Café. Dunno McManus and Kitter Murray were standing outside.

"Well."

"Hi Red."

"Who's in?"

"Nobody, Anto's on, but none of the boys are here," replied Dunno.

"Did you see Po on your travels?" asked Red.

"He was here earlier and said he'd be back," said Kitter.

"…and talk of the Devil…" Kitter nodded towards the other side of the road.

It was Po with Ginger McVerry.

"Hi Red, have ya any money?" asked Po.

"No…why?"

"Mom gave me money yesterday to get a Mass card for old Johnny McCall. I spent it."

"We'll get one later from somewhere," said Red unconcerned.

"Have you been up ta the wake yet?" Po asked Red.

"No, but I have ta go there sometime today."

"I'll go with ya, don't wanna go up there on my own," muttered Po.

"Ya afraid auld Johnny might get up and grab ya," laughed Dunno.

"Ya right Dunno, go bite yourself."

"I was gonna see a match out in the Meadow tonight between Shamrocks and Bessbrook United," said Red to Po.

"Yeah, heard about that one, I'll go with ya and we'll go up ta the wake after."

Later that day Red and Po watched Bessbrook United beat Shamrocks 2 – 1 in a very hard fought and tight match. When the match was over as arranged, they started off towards High Street and Johnny McCall's wake.

"Where did ya get the Mass Card?" Po asked Red.

"The one I gave ya?"

"Yeah."

"Ma Aunt Josie called up ta the house. She didn't even know auld Johnny but felt she should get a card anyways. It's the one she gave me the money for that ya got."

"They get hundreds of them, don't they?"

"That's for sure, the priests make a fortune."

They had arrived at McCall's house on High Street about nine thirty. The house was packed to overflowing with people spilling out onto the street. Two of the family members were positioned at the door to greet the mourners. Red knew both well. One was Peter, Johnny's eldest son and the other was the second son, Mike.

Red and Po shook hands with both and chatted for a few minutes.

"Well, he had been very ill for a long time," said Peter.

"Yeah, I know Pete, but it was still very sudden though," said Po.

"That it was…Oh, have you met Jonathan?"

A tall man had just arrived from inside the house.

Red swallowed hard. He felt the blood draining from his face. He looked at Po who was standing with his mouth open. Jonathan laughed a deep hearty laugh and placed his hand on Red's shoulder. "Ya don't have ta say anythin', I know! I've been gettin' the same reaction all day from people arriving here."

Red licked his now dry lips, "But ya…"

"I know, I look just like him. Johnny was my identical twin."

"Christ, I thought it was Johnny there for a minute," said Po getting his breath back.

Jonathan laughed. "Very few people know me here, I've lived in England all my life and I've given a few of them quite a shock today."

After the two had been to see Johnny laid out in his coffin in the upstairs front room, said a prayer, and placed the Mass cards in the coffin beside him, they came down stairs to be greeted by Johnny's daughter Rhoda. After giving her their condolences they were ushered into the living room to speak to Johnny's wife. Mrs. McCall was seated in a great cushioned sofa by the window surrounded by neighbours and friends. Red approached and offered his hand.

"I was very sorry to hear about Johnny Mrs. McCall," he said softly.

"Thank you very much son. You're young Morgan from Castle Street, aren't you?"

"My God look at the size of him," interrupted Mrs. Rooney seated next to Mrs. McCall. "I used to change his nappies ya know," she laughed. "Do ya remember me a'tall?"

"Indeed I do Mrs. Rooney."

"It wouldn't do for me ta change ya now would it?"

"Well I wouldn't say that Mrs. Rooney, sure ya had great soft hands."

This brought a rattle of laughter from the listening audience.

"Get out of it ya bad ruffian, sure ya'll make me blush next."

"Take a lot to make you blush Mary," piped in Mrs. Jones seated across the room. The ribbing went on for a few minutes and Red and Po said their goodbyes.

On the way down High Street Po brought up the subject of Johnny's twin brother.

"I tell ya Red, I nearly shit when I saw him."

"I know what ya mean, I couldn't believe it ma own self, I thought I was seein' things."

They arrived at Uncle Luigi's and began telling Anto about the wake and of course Johnny's brother. Anto sat in the snug for a while deep in thought.

"Ya know Red, we could have some fun with this one."

"What ya mean?"

"Who is the dopiest, most gullible and stupidest one of the boys?"

"Jasus, that would be a toss up," put in Po.

"It would ya know…what about Dunno?"

"Much of a muchness far as I'm concerned," said Red.

"Right, this is the plan."

The three huddled together and in a short space of time the plot was hatched.

Later that night the whole gang was there but Anto had isolated Dunno by getting him to do some work out the back.

"Red, you come out the back with me and we'll start the ball rolling with Dunno."

"Sure ya don't need me, you can do it."

"No way, ya could sell ice to the Eskimos. He'll believe you before me, that's for sure."

The two of them started out the back.

"I've already started him goin' a bit, so ya just follow me, right?"

Red smiled and nodded.

"Yo Dunno," shouted Anto.

"Well, what's the craic?"

"Hi Dunno," greeted Red.

"I have all the spuds packed away Anto."

"Jasus Dunno sure you're nothin' short of deadly. It would've taken me all night to do that. He's the man, isn't he Red?"

"That he is, that he is."

They sat down on some bags of potatoes and Anto handed round a pack of John Player cigarettes.

"Hey, where are ya all?" It was the voice of Shifty McShane.

"Out here," said Anto.

Shifty arrived, demanded a cigarette and sat down.

"So, as I was tellin' ya earlier, if ya don't believe me, ask Red," said Anto.

"That's the biggest load of shit I've ever heard," said Dunno.

"What's this?" asked Red.

"Ok, look, you're well up on legend and old wives tales and the like, aren't ya Red?"

"Suppose…maybe, why?"

"Did ya ever come across the legend of the 'Dead Man's Last Drink' a'tall?"

"Ach aye, sure that's as old as the hills."

"It's all a load of shit, that's what it is," put in Dunno.

"What's this?" asked Shifty.

"Tell them Red, you know it better than me," chirped Anto.

"Well, let's see if I can remember it all. The night before the dead man is buried, it's traditional for his family, well the men that is, ta go ta his favourite pub and have a drink ta him, ya know, a toast. They even put a pint up on the bar for him."

"Yeah, so?"

"Well, as the story goes, the dead man's spirit joins them for one last drink. I have heard it said many times that the dead man was seen drinking in the pub with the people there and they didn't know it."

"That's stupid."

"Ah, but there we find the trick of the dead."

"What de ya mean?"

"Well, even though they're all talkin' ta him, they're under a sort a spell and they don't know it. Next day they have forgotten all about it."

"I've heard tall stories before Red, but that one takes the biscuit," said Shifty.

"Hey, I'm not askin' ya ta believe it, I'm just tellin' ya what the legend is."

"How could ya believe a load like that?" asked Dunno.

"My Uncle Pajoe was walkin' past a pub one night when a wake crowd was comin' out. He swears the dead man was in the middle of them and one even had an arm around his shoulders. Next day he was talking ta them and when he told them what he saw, they laughed at him and told him he was crazy," said Red as seriously as he could.

"Jasus, that's friggin' weird, whaddya say Shifty?" asked Dunno.

"Weird? Yeah, suppose, but I don't believe it."

Just then, as if on cue, Po arrived. When he was filled in on the conversation so far he said.

"Sure I know all about that. My dad has been to a few dead man's last drinks."

"Holy shit, I have it," shouted Anto standing up and slapping his hands on his head.

"What?" asked Red.

"Red, where did Johnny McCall drink, what was his local?"

"Ah, Murtagh's Bar on Castle Street, why?"

"Think about it ya ejits. This is the last night of the Wake, right? Johnny is getting himself buried in the mornin'."

Anto let it soak in for a minute.

"Ya get it?"

"Jasus, he's right," said Po looking at Shifty.

"Johnny's ghost might be in Murtagh's tonight."

"Are ya game Red, will we go up there at closin' time and hide behind Carroll's old wall and watch them comin' out?"

"Are you boys goin'?" Red looked at Dunno and Shifty.

"Why not, if it's only ta prove that you lot are talkin' through your arses."

Later that night, about twelve thirty, Red, Anto, Po, Shifty and Dunno were behind Carroll's old wall which was almost opposite Murtagh's Pub. Po had already stuck his head around the door of the pub to ensure that all the men from the wake were there and they were.

"What time will they be comin' out Anto?" asked Dunno.

"Anytime now," whispered Anto.

"This is a total waste of time ya know," whispered Shifty.

"Shush, the door's openin' now," said Po.

"Oh my God, I don't believe it, I can see Johnny," said Red making the sign of the cross.

"I can see him too," said Po.

"That's him all right, I'd know him anywhere, Jasus Christ," said Anto.
"It's him, oh my God, it's Johnny's ghost, it's him, it's really him."
Moments later realisation followed closely by panic set in to both Shifty and Dunno.
"Ahaaaaa…" there was a rustling and movement beside Red as two bodies took off as fast as their legs could take them screaming at the top of their voices.

Outside the pub, Jonathan McCall stopped to see what the commotion was across the road.
"What on earth's going on over there?"
"Just some kids messin' about I expect," said one of the men.
"Christ, the screams of them…you'd think they'd seen a ghost!"

End

The Mystery Tour

1960

Paddy Morgan, Red's grandfather, was standing on the step of the old green and white Ulster Transport Authority bus that he'd hired for the day. He was dressed in his Sunday clothes, a dark brown jacket and black trousers, the familiar flat cap and a blue and grey thin cotton scarf all of which had seen better days. Paddy was engrossed in the passenger list in his hands. He was making sure that everyone who had paid for the trip was on board.

It was a Saturday morning in mid July that, for once, lived up to its summer ranking. It was a beautiful day and the sun had an uncluttered view of this small part of the earth. Paddy scanned all the faces on the bus, nodding and smiling at some as he made his mental count. He had been doing this monthly trip for more than fifteen years. In fact, he had inherited it from his father. It had become a family tradition. When he was satisfied, he turned to the driver, "Well, as far as I can see, everybody's here."

"So, we're on our way then," said the driver as he began his preparations for moving off.

The great plan was that every other month the trip would be called a 'Mystery Tour'. This simply meant that no one knew the destination of the trip, save Paddy and the driver. Red hated these trips but was forced to go by his mom and dad. He always hoped that Po's parents would be going and then he knew for sure that Po would be forced to go as well. On this day Po was indeed there, so it might not be too boring after all. They were both sitting together near the front of the bus. A few more of the gang were also there with their parents. Red noted the presence of Naffy McKay, Jumpy Jones, Blackie Havern and Boots Markey. They were on their way. The old bus trundled along Castle Street, onto Bridge Street and headed for the Dublin Road.

"Where do ya think we're goin'?" Po asked looking out the window.
"Well, if ya remember, the last mystery tour ended up in Dundrum. Since we're on the Dublin Road, headin' south, it looks like Blackrock or maybe Clogherhead."
"I hate Blackrock, there's frig all ta do there."

Just under an hour later Red knew his guess was right, as the bus pulled into a small car park in Clogherhead, Co. Louth.
"Right, everybody, now listen for a minute," came the loud voice of Paddy Morgan from the front of the bus.
"We'll be leavin' for home at nine o'clock, and not a minute later. If you're not here, we're not waitin'. "

With a lot of fussing from the ladies and 'hurry ups' from the men the bus emptied. The great divide or separation began for most. The women's immediate aims were, toilets, shops, food, more shops, beach and home. For the men it was pub, drink, more drink, sing song, more drink and home.

Po and Red got instructions from their mothers...no this, no that, and no the other. They had heard it all before and just nodded. In a short time the boys had separated themselves from what they called the 'cobweb mob' and were on their way as far as possible from moms and dads. They had received pocket money from mom who complained bitterly about the fact that dad had not given them any money. They had heard the same complaints from dad ten minutes earlier.

First ports of call were the numerous amusement arcades. With half the pocket money dispensed with trying to win prizes they were back on the street heading for the beach. When they found a nice spot, the lads changed into their swimwear and headed for the sea. After much splashing and diving, jumping and falling, and in some cases swimming, most had returned to the laid out towels and began to enjoy the hot summer sun. So, the first of mom's rules was broken…'don't be lyin' in the sun'. This subject was addressed by Po.

"Ya know what I was wonderin', do moms and dads have a bunch of do's and don'ts for their kids that they add to every year, or do they just make them up as they go along?"

"My mom adds to them every week," added in Boots Markey.

"So does mine," said Jumpy Jones.

"My da's worse than my mom," said Blackie Havern.

"He never stops with the do's and don'ts."

"I suppose they have ta, it's probably in their weddin' contract. If they don't tell us what ta do and what not ta do, they get fined," mused Jumpy.

An hour later the boys were getting urgent signals from their stomachs. The search for moms with purses began in earnest and once found, the gang bought fish and chips and lemonade.

Later in the afternoon they decided to walk the length of the beach. Sitting or lying in the sun, building sand castles, playing football, messing about in the water, had all lost its appeal. On their journey, they came across some rocks jutting out into the sea. This seemed a place where some fun could be had and they all began to run at once as if injected with the same thought. After an initial inspection of the rocks, Red heard the voice of Boots Markey. "Hey lads, look what I found."

He climbed to the top of the rocks to get a better view. On the other side were Boots and Blackie standing in a small row boat which had been tied to a large rock. Blackie was standing in the bow with his hand shading his eyes looking out to sea as if he were captain. After all were on board Jumpy presented what he thought was a bright idea.

"She has oars and everythin', lets take her out for a spin?" he suggested.

"Great idea," agreed Naffy.

"No way, I'm not goin' out there in this," said Po.

"Count me out too," said Red.

"Me too," added Blackie.

"Bunch of wee girls, come on Naffy, let's get it in the sea."

"Come on boys, if you're all afraid ta go out at least give us a push to get it in the water," said Boots standing in the boat with his hands on his hips. They all agreed and began the task of launching the boat. It wasn't as easy as first supposed. Despite the weight, they eventually moved the craft into the sea. The boat was launched and Boots and Jumpy had the oars in operation…just not at the same time and the boat turned one way then the other. Naffy was acting as captain. After some instructions from the beach crew they finally began pulling the oars together until the boat took a straighter course out to sea.

"Don't go out too far," shouted Red from between cupped hands.

The boys got the hang of 'sculling' and the boat was moving quite quickly. When it was about three hundred yards from the beach, Boots stood up to wave. As he did so, he let go of his oar which slipped into the sea and took up sailing on its own…away from the boat that was now caught in a current and was moving out to sea without any help from those on board. Boots, Jumpy and Naffy had now realised what was happening and began shouting for help from those on shore. The three boys saw everything and began to realise their friends were in serious trouble.

"What'll we do?" pleaded Po.

"Can we swim out there?" asked Blackie.

"No way," said Red. "We'd end up in trouble too."

"What'll we do?"

"I think we should get help," piped in Blackie.

"That's the best move, you're the fastest runner Po, go ta the pub and get the dads quick as ya can." Po took off running down the beach at top speed. He reached the pub in under five minutes and breathlessly relayed the situation to the men there. They followed Po back to the beach where Red and Blackie were still standing. The boat was now about a thousand yards out.

Naffy's dad and two other men took off their shoes and jackets and began wading out towards the boat. Red looked at his dad who was now standing beside him.

"Will they be able ta swim out that far?"

"Hopefully they won't need to, it's a high beach," he answered still out of breath from his run.

"What's a high beach Dad?" asked Red.

"Well it means that the beach doesn't drop steeply, ya would need ta walk out there a mile before the water would cover your head."

The men finally reached the boat. Naffy's dad was so glad to see him he could be seen patting the back of Naffy's head with his open hand almost knocking him into the sea. The water was just above their waists. Po pulled Red to one side.

"Them friggin' ejits could've got out of the boat and pulled it ashore."

"I can friggin' see that."

"They're all dead for sure, they'll be hammered."

"I'm sure glad we didn't go out with them."

Red felt a blinding crash on the back of his head. He immediately realised it had been caused by his father's right hand.

"What did ya think ya were doin' lettin' them go out in that boat?"

Po's dad was reciting the same theme to Po.

Twenty minutes later the beach was a hive of activity. The women had now arrived. The boys and the boat were back on shore and the mom's were practising their slapping skills on the boy's heads with great regularity. The men, dressed in beach towels, were wringing the sea out of their pants.

Later that evening on the bus home, Red and Po were again seated together. Red stood up to look for Naffy, Jumpy and Boots who were seated in the back just ahead of their parents. They were silent having been told that one word from any of them would lead to imminent death.

"Some trip, eh?" whispered Po. Red giggled.

"Sure was, for Popeye, Black Beard and Long John Silver back there." They both began giggling only to incur instant 'mom slapping' directly on the back of their heads. 'Why do they never miss?' thought Red.

"Do ya think it's funny, do ya?" said Po's mom through her teeth.

"I'll funny ya," said Red's mom with another well aimed slap.

All the adventurers arrived home safely after another wonderful Mystery Tour. Perhaps next time there would be a little excitement for a change.

End

The All Ireland Final

1960

At eight-thirty Sunday morning, Edward Street Railway Station in Newry was packed to capacity with red and black clad County Down supporters. It was a colourful scene as they gathered for the trip to Dublin for the All Ireland Final.

Never before had a team from Northern Ireland won the Final and hopes were high that 1960 would be their year. Teams from the North made it to the Semi Finals and sometimes the Final, but they always fell short against the might of the great teams from the Republic like Dublin, Kerry, Cork, Offaly, and Galway.

Nearly the whole gang were there, Red, Anto, Po, Kitter, Blackie, Dunno, Bishop, Shifty and Jumpy. They gathered near the end of the platform, the only remaining available space.

"Did ya all get your instructions this mornin' from mommy and daddy boys?"

Po held his arms in the air as if directing them.

"Yes Po," they all answered.

"And were ya told that there'd be none of this..?"

"Yes Po."

"And were ya told there'd be none of that..?"

"Yes Po."

"And were ya told there'd definitely be none of…"

"The other," they all shouted.

They broke into song as they made a circle, with arms around each other's shoulders…

"We don't care whether we win or lose or draw,
Damn the hair we care,
For we only know that there's goin' to be a match
And all the Down men will be there!"

This was followed by loud cheering, both for the song and because they noticed the special football train arriving. When all were on board and seated, the train left the station for Ireland's capital, Dublin.

It took almost two hours to cover the sixty five mile journey. The train made a stop at Gorawood Station, three miles north of Newry, where the engine was detached, turned around and reattached at the other end for the journey south. They arrived at Amiens Street Station in Dublin at ten-thirty. The match ground, Croke Park, was about two miles from the station and they had plenty of time to walk since kick off wasn't until three-thirty in the afternoon.

"Hey Red, where's O'Connell Street?" asked Kitter knowing Red had been to Dublin before. Red pointed, "Just straight ahead at the top of that street."

"Let's go there first, I wanna see Nelson's Pillar," pleaded Dunno.

The gang arrived at O'Connell Street and stood looking in amazement not only at its size, but also at the thousands of people and vehicles using it. This was a whole new world for the lads who took it all in, wide-eyed and open-mouthed.

"Jasus Christ! It's ten times bigger than I thought," commented Dunno.

"It's unbelievable, isn't it?" joined Kitter.

"Red, is that Nelson's Pillar there?" asked Shifty.

"Yep, that's it all right. Just for your information it's one hundred and twenty feet high, not countin' himself on top."

"Jasus, can we go ta the top now?" asked Blackie.

"I suppose, but I'm not goin'. I've been up there before and I can tell ya, it's hard work gettin' up, plus there's probably hundreds in the queue."

"I want ta go anyways," continued Blackie. "Who's with me?"

A chorus of 'Me, Me' followed.

"Red, how'll we get ta the football ground if we get lost?"

"Ya see all them guys with red and black flags, and those ones with green, white and gold? Well, they're all goin' ta the match, if ya follow them ya'll get there. Ya got your tickets so we'll meet up inside, we're all seated together in the Cusack Stand anyways."

A few minutes later Red, Po and Anto were on their own.

"So what'll we do ta pass the time? We've got about three hours ta kill," said Po.

"I got a cousin who has a place on Camden Street. Why don't we go there and get somethin' ta eat?" suggested Anto.

"Best suggestion I've heard all day," replied Red.

"I agree with your man," added Po nodding at Red. He got a punch on the arm for his cheek.

Fifteen minutes later they were in Malinie's Café on Camden Street, tucking into a large plate of sausage, egg and chips accompanied by mugs of tea. When they'd finished and had spent a little time chatting with Anto's cousin and some of the staff, they made their way back to O'Connell Street. By this time the street was a mass of colour displayed by the thousands of fans going to the match. The boys bought flags from a street seller and went off toward Drumcondra, and Croke Park.

As they approached the stadium the crowds thickened. They met up with some Kerry fans who began bantering and good natured teasing. They walked with them engrossed in conversation about the players on both sides and this made the two mile walk pass quickly. Soon they found themselves queuing up at the Cusack Stand side of the ground with tickets in hand. The excitement grew as they passed through the turnstile. After being directed to the middle entrance of the Cusack Stand, they climbed to the top tier and walked through the passageway to behold the breathtaking spectacle that was the inside of Croke Park. The noise emanating from the assembled crowd was deafening. The official attendance was given to be 87,768 but the unofficial total was said to be nearer 95,000! A massive roar from the crowd sent shivers up their spines. They had to stand to see what was happening. The two teams, Kerry and Down had come onto the pitch.

After the most exciting one and a half hours of their lives, the referee blew the final whistle. The match was over. Down were the All Ireland Champions with a massive score of 2 -10 to 0 – 8. The Down fans were ecstatic. They were kissing, dancing, crying and some just sitting with their heads in their hands unable to take in the emotion of it all. The excited fans had swarmed onto the pitch and were carrying the Down team shoulder high to the Hogan Stand at the other side of the ground. There, the President of Ireland would present Down with the 'Sam Maguire Cup'.

It took the boys almost thirty minutes to get to ground level. They had again made arrangements to meet and this time it was to be at Amiens Street Station at eight-thirty. The train home was leaving at nine o'clock. As expected, they did get separated and Po and Red were on their own. Just as they got to within fifty yards of the exit, a bottleneck at the gate was making movement difficult. Everyone was squeezed tightly together and moving very slowly. Just in front of Red a woman seemed to be having problems. She began to stumble and fall and Red grabbed her as best he could and Po, aware of what was happening pushed forward to help Red hold her up. Two of the Stadium marshals pushed their way through the crowd to help. They managed to get the woman, with the help of a couple of hefty Kerrymen, to one side of the heaving throng.
"Take her this way," said one of the marshals to Red. By this time the middle-aged woman, had fainted and needed to be carried. Between Red, Po and the two marshals they moved the woman away from the crowd in the direction of the Hogan Stand.
"There's no point tryin' ta get her ta the First Aid Room in the Cusack, we'd never get through," said one of the marshals.

"I agree, it would be an easier job now if we took her through the staff entrance to the First Aid Room in the Hogan."

After gently laying the woman on the ground, one of the men produced a large bunch of keys and opened the door. They carried the woman into a long dark echoing corridor which seemed to go on forever. Red's arms were aching with the weight of her. They had to stop twice to get a breather. Eventually they reached another door which Red could see led to the First Aid Room. In fact, it was more like a hospital ward. The place was a hive of activity with tending nurses, doctors and Knight's of Malta in grey uniforms. A nurse directed them to place the lady on a treatment table, which they did with some relief, giving all their aching arms some respite.

"Thanks lads, what happened to her?" asked the nurse.

One of the men explained what happened.

"You two should be proud of yourselves. If you hadn't grabbed her and she'd gone down, she could have been trampled to death," responded the nurse.

"Now take yourselves outside, out of the way, and again thanks for your help."

When they were back in the corridor, one of the marshals turned to Red.

"You two did a great job there. Where ya from?"

"Newry."

"Sure I know it well. My sister married a Bessbrook man."

The other one butted in.

"Would yis like a cuppa lads?"

"Love one," said Po.

"Come on then and we'll see what we can do, maybe even get ya a sandwich as well. Can't let our two heroes go home to Newry sayin' that Dubliners are a miserable lot, now can we?"

Red and Po followed the two men along the corridor. There were more people about now. They arrived at a door which had two large men standing on guard outside. One of the marshals had a quick word and the door was opened to allow admittance. When they got inside they found themselves in a large dining hall with many people milling about, drinking tea and eating sandwiches from two long, well stocked tables. "There ya go lads, help yourselves. We have ta go back ta work. Hope we meet again. Good luck to ya," the two men shook hands with Red and Po, and left.

"Jasus, this is great, isn't it, come on, let's get some food," said Po moving to one of the tables. A few minutes later, each with a plate packed high with buns, cakes, and sandwiches, plus a large mug of tea, found some empty seats and made themselves comfortable.

"Are you the two lads that helped the lady in the crowd?" came a voice from behind. Red turned his head and looked up. He almost choked on his sandwich when he found himself looking into the face of Kevin Mussen, Captain of the Down Team.
"Yes Sir, that was us," stammered Red.
"Never mind the Sir, Kevin will do."
"Sorry Sir, a mean Kevin."
Red looked at Po who was sitting open mouthed.
"I was talking to the two marshals at the door and they told me what happened. I hear ya did a great job. Come on over here and I'll introduce you to the team."
Tea and buns were forgotten as Po and Red followed Kevin to the other end of the room, where sitting around two large tables were the All Ireland Champions. Red and Po were introduced to them all. It was a dream come true for Red. Shaking hands with Tony Hadden, Paddy Docherty, Sean O'Neil, Kevin O'Neill, Breen Morgan, James McCarten and others, would become a memory that would remain with him forever.
"Have you boys got Match Programmes?" asked Paddy Docherty.
Both reached into their pockets and produced the programmes that were handed around for the team to sign. It was now almost eight o'clock, but time was the last thing Red and Po had on their minds.
"Did you come by train?" Kevin Mussen asked Po.
"Yes, we have to be at the station by eight thirty."
Kevin called to someone at the other side of the room.
"What time are we leaving for the Hotel?"

"In ten minutes," came the reply.

"There ya go, problem solved. You can come with us as far as O'Connell Street and sure Amiens Street's only a stones throw from there."

"That would be great, thanks very much Kevin."

"No problem."

Thirty minutes later they were entering Amiens Street Station which was a heaving mass of jubilant singing and dancing Down fans. They found their train and got on board. The rest of the gang, already there, had kept seats for them.

Soon the train was on its way. The conversation during the return trip was, as expected, about Down's great victory, who played well, who scored, who nearly did, who was fouled, and who was the man of the match.

"You two aren't saying much, did ya not have a good time?" asked Kitter.

"Sure we did, we had a great time," answered Po.

"We got ta see the team passing in the bus on the way to their hotel, and they waved at us. Did ya see them?"

"Sort of," said Red smiling.

Red and Po exchanged glances. They both reached into their inside pockets and took out their Match Programmes.

"Do ya know, I lost my programme," complained Dunno.

"Well, we wouldn't want ta lose these ones, would we Red?" asked Po.

"Too right, these are worth a small fortune for sure."

"What do ya mean?" asked Kitter.

Red handed him the programme.

"Jasus Christ, I don't believe it!"

"They've only got the autographs of the whole friggin' team."

"What?" came the unanimous response.

The Match Programmes were inspected by everyone in the carriage. A man even offered them twenty pounds for one. Red and Po sat back with self satisfied grins on their faces. It had been quite a day. Going home, an extra colour was evident on the train. The black and red Down colours and the green of envy!

End

The Smugglers

1960

The town of Newry is situated some three miles from the border with the Republic of Ireland. The smuggling of goods from South to North and vice versa has been part of people's lives in the area for many years. It was never looked upon as a crime as such by the people of Newry and its surrounding districts, but more as a simple way of making a few extra shillings for hard up families in the area. The practice was widespread and kept the customs people busy due to the great number of un-approved roads between North and South. In some cases a house was in the north of Ireland and the garden was in the south, or a pub had its Bar in the north and its Lounge in the south.

Minnie O'Hare was a lady well into her seventies who made her money from smuggling cigarettes from Dundalk to Newry three times a week. This was done by stuffing the packets of cigarettes into a specially made bodice she wore that had vertical panels sewn in. When full, each panel would hold five packets of twenty cigarettes. There were twelve panels in the bodice, therefore, on every trip she made, she carried twelve hundred cigarettes. During the many years Minnie did this she was never once caught by customs. Every Monday, Wednesday and Friday Minnie would arrive at Red Morgan's house on Castle Street at four thirty. She would, with the help of Red's mom or grandmother, unpack the cigarettes from her bodice and deliver them to local shops for sale. She made enough money to pay for her trip, give Red's family a few shillings and a tidy sum for under the mattress.

One Sunday afternoon Minnie's son arrived at Red's house to inform them that his mom was ill and would be laid up that coming Monday. Red's mom agreed to take her place for a small fee. Red and Po were employed as 'customs distractions' for the trip and also to carry some 'illegal goods' themselves. They had done this in the past using Red's old football. The ball was unlaced and up to twenty packs of cigarettes were pushed inside. The ball was then laced back up again and it was Red's job to sit playing with it on the way through customs.

When Po came along, he would carry butter for his mom which was also much cheaper at that time in the south. His method was to have the butter packed into a false bottom in a football kit bag. On this particular day however, Po had two extra packets of butter which he packed neatly inside his shirt.

The journey was uneventful from Dundalk until they reached the border. This is where the customs men would get on the bus and check some bags and ask some questions like, 'Are you carrying any goods which might be liable for customs duty?' to which the answer of course, was always, 'no'.

Po had been sitting at the window next to Red who was just across the aisle from Mrs. Morgan who sat on the outside seat. Red noticed that Po had been unusually quiet over this past couple of miles and also noted that he was looking quite pale.

"Are you ok?" Red whispered.
"Shush," was the only reply.
"What's wrong?"
"Tell ya later, shush will ya."

Red just shrugged his shoulders and continued throwing the ball up and down in his hands.

The customs man had now come onto the bus and was sharing a joke it seemed with the bus conductor. He then started his walk along the bus stopping to check a bag or ask a question, sometimes saying hello to people he knew. He passed Red and Po's seat without a word and continued to the front of the bus, turned and walked back to the exit. Saying goodbye, he left the bus and they were soon on their way again on the final three miles to Newry. Red looked at Po again.

"Are ya goin' ta tell me what's up?" he asked.

"No, a said a would tell ya later, right?" Po snapped impatiently.

"Right then, moody wee bugger."

The bus pulled into its assigned stopping place on the Mall and the passengers began to exit. Red's mom stood up and motioned him forward. Po did not move. Red looked at his mom and told her to go ahead of him. When almost all the passengers on the bus had disembarked Red spoke to Po.

"Are ya right?"

"Go you on ahead; I'll follow ya in a minute."

Red stood up and left the bus. Once outside he handed the ball to his waiting mom. She gave him a half crown which she had already taken from her purse and before leaving, warned him not to be late for his tea.

Red looked up in time to see Po exiting the bus. He noticed Po seemed to be making a determined effort to hide his groin area with his coat.

"Right you, what's goin' on?"

"Can't ya guess dopey?" snapped Po.

"No a can't. What's the problem?"

"The friggin' butter's the friggin' problem."

"The butter?"

"The whorin' butter."

"So what's wrong with the whorin' butter?" Red could not stop himself smiling.

"I forgot somethin' didn't I?"

"Ok, I'll ask then. What did ya forget Po," Red asked sarcastically.

"Now listen Morgan, this is not ta go any further, right?"

"What isn't?"

"If a tell ya, it's between you and me, right?"

"As if I would tell anyone."

"I know ya, ya bastard, remember?"

"Will ya tell me for Christ's sake, will ya?"

"Well, like a said, I forgot somethin'."

"Ok, what?"

Po removed his coat from in front of his groin area to show a large stain covering the complete front of his once grey trousers.

"Jasus, ya pissed yourself."

Po punched Red in the chest.

"No I friggin' didn't ya weirdo."

"What's that then?"

"I forgot about whorin' body heat didn't I. The stupid butter melted and run down."

Red had to sit down on the wall beside the bus stop. He literally could not stand up. He felt the tears running down his face and the pain in his sides was growing stronger. Every time Po spoke he was making matters worse.

"Oh yeah, go on then ya bastard, have a good laugh."

"Stop, please, I'm beggin' Po, stop."

So ended yet another exciting day in Red and Po's life. Red was threatened that if he ever told anyone he would die a slow and very painful death. No one can be sure if he ever did break the promise but for a long time Red's new nickname for Po left people with puzzled looks on their faces.

'Butter Balls!'

End

Market Day

1960

Red knocked on Po's door which was opened by his mom.

"Hi Red."

"Hello Mrs. Hillen, is he in?"

"In his room I think, come in."

Red followed Mrs. Hillen through the hall to the bottom of the stairs.

"Go on up Red."

Red climbed the stairs three at a time and turned at the top landing to go to Po's room. He had to pass the open door to the bedroom of Po's sister and what he saw stopped him in his tracks.

Po was standing on a small stool. He wore a yellow full length dress and his sister, Maeve, was kneeling in front of him.

"Oh my God," commented Red entering the room.

"Jasus," said Po, looking up at the ceiling, "This is all I need."

"Po, I have ta say, I've never seen ya look so lovely."

"Hi Red," mumbled Po's sister, her mouth full of pins.

"Maeve, Po really suits yellow, doesn't he? What colour shoes are ya wearin' with that Po?"

Po reached behind him to a bookshelf, grabbed a paperback and threw it at Red's grinning face. Red ducked the missile and continued his taunting.

"Po," shouted Maeve, "Stay still will ya?"

"Ya know, I have ta tell ya. With a dress like that, Po, you'll have ta be careful about the bra and panties ya wear with it."

"I'm not gonna answer ya Morgan. Ya'll not get to me, no way."

"Right, I'm finished, now be very careful taking it off," Maeve instructed.

"Will I turn my back?" asked Red.

Po just gave him an angry glance. Moments later they were sitting on Po's bed.

"It's a good job ya left the door open. I wouldn't want anyone gettin' the wrong idea. By the by, when did ya turn into a fruit? I never suspected."

"You won't let this go will ya, ya bastard?"

"Nope, would you?"

"Nope," smiled Po "What did ya call for anyways?"

"Johnny the Limp, in the Market? Well, he wants a hand, loadin' his stuff, to get it ta the train this afternoon…about four-thirty. Ya up for it?"

"Yeah, why not."

At four thirty that afternoon, Red and Po were helping Johnny the Limp pack up his stall in Newry Market. He, like most of the other stall holders, was from Belfast. They transported their wares, and themselves, by train making use of Dublin Bridge Station which was just a few hundred yards from the Market. They used large four by three foot baskets, to carry their stuff, on long lugged wheelbarrows, too and from the trains. Most Saturdays Johnny the Limp had his son with him, but on this day he didn't. He would give Red a half crown to pack his wares of second-hand men's clothing, and transport them to the Railway Station.

Red and Po were almost finished when Red heard someone shout his name. He looked around to see one of his neighbour's kids, little Joey Smith. Joey was ten years old and small for his age.

"Red, hide me, will ya?"

"What?"

"We're playin' Tig."

"Where can I hide ya?"

"In one of them baskets," suggested Po.

"Ok," Red opened the lid of a half filled basket, "Get in."

They noted other kids running around the Market in search of Joey who was obviously the last to be caught.

Po bent down and lifted the lid on the basket.

"You ok in there?" he asked Joey.

"Yeah, are the boys still lookin' for me?"

"They are."

Joey giggled.

"Joey, we have ta take these baskets to Dublin Bridge. You stay in there and we'll let ya out at the station, ok?"

"Ok," came the muffled reply.

Red got the barrow lip under the basket containing Joey and they loaded another on top.

"So are we right Sylvia?"

"Sylvia?"

"Yeah, Sylvia. I think it suits ya better. Po's a wee bit too masculine ya know."

"Ya bastard, are ya gonna keep this up all day?"

"All year."

"Friggin' bastard."

"Yes dear."

Po took a swing at Red but missed. They reached the railway station ten minutes later and were stacking baskets when they heard the screech of car tyres. They both ran to the front of the station to see a driver standing by his car shaking his fist at some young kids who had run across the road in front of him. Red and Po returned to the station platform and continued to load the last of the baskets on the 5.15pm Belfast Express. On the way back to Hill Street, each jingling the one shilling and three pence they got from Johnny the Limp, they were in a good mood. Po was going on about some girl he had seen standing outside Woolworth. From the way he was describing her, Red was beginning to think Po had a notebook with him and jotted down every detail.

"So why didn't ya just go over and ask her out then if she was so beautiful?"
"Piss off, ya can't do that, not without knowin' her."
"Sure with your good looks, and devastatin' personality, she would'a just fallen into your arms," smirked Red.
"Yeah, right. Anyway, as I was sayin', I think she's a cousin of Jackie Rooney."
"Hmmm," Red answered, his interest waning.
"Jasus."
"What."
"Joey!"
"What for Christ's sake?"
"Frig me!"
"What? What?"
"Joey…Joey!"
"Jasus! We forgot about him! What'll we do?"
"I don't know, let me think a minute."
"The train's well gone by now."
"I know, I know!"
"Ok now, let's stay calm. Who do we know has a car?"
"Anto's Uncle Roberto."
"Come on."

Both raced at top speed to Uncle Luigi's Café. They found Roberto working behind the Ice Cream counter. While listening to Red and Po, Roberto threw off his apron and all three rushed across the road to his parked car.
"Now you're sure the train stops at Gorawood Red?"
"Positive."
"It stops there for about twenty minutes ta let the Dublin train pass before it heads off for Belfast."

Ten minutes later they were pulling into Gorawood Railway Station about three miles north of Newry. They ran to the platform and found that the Belfast Express was still standing there. Po spied a guard at the far end of the platform. Following another explanation of circumstances, the guard went to the freight car filled with baskets and opened it. With four of them searching, the basket in question was found quickly. Joey was still hiding inside, in fact, he was fast asleep.

Back in Newry, outside Uncle Luigi's, Red and Po thanked Roberto for all his help and offered him money for petrol. Roberto turned down the offer and said he was happy enough to be of help, but gave Red and Po a finger shaking lecture about putting Joey in the basket in the first place.

Red turned to Joey.

"Now we'll not say a word about this to anyone, so don't you."

"I know, I'd get into bad trouble, wouldn't I?"

"Yeah, ya would for sure," replied Po.

Joey thought for a moment, and looked up at Red smiling.

"But come ta think of it, so would you Red, have ya any money?"

"Get outta here ya wee brat!" he shouted as Joey took off with Red's kick brushing his backside.

"Another exciting day, huh?" stated Red.

"Yep."

"A lost wee boy, a near accident and a mate who turned out to be a fruit."

Red took off with Po in pursuit and using language not fit for the ears of decent society.

End

The Camping Trip

1960

"Now, are ya sure?" Po asked Bishop Keenan.

"Look, I've checked three times, we have everything."

"I know ya have everything Bishop, but are ya sure?" asked Po.

"Piss off."

"Charmin' isn't he?" said Po to Red and Shifty McShane.

"Charmin'," was the dual reply.

"Ok then, so let's go."

Six of the boys were planning to go on a camping trip in the Mourne Mountains. They decided that since none of them, other than Anto, had ever camped before they should have a trial run. On this weekend, four of them were going to camp at the site of an old abandoned granite quarry called 'The Blue Motion' which was just off Courtney Hill in Newry. Why it was called 'Blue Motion' no one ever knew since the water that filled it was in fact green. The quarry was abandoned when workers hit an underground river and it filled up never to be of any use again. Many swimmers and divers lost their lives in the Blue Motion. It was said that if you got caught up in the undercurrents of the river you could be carried underground and lost forever. In fact, as the local stories go, the bodies of people drowned in the quarry were never recovered. With this being widespread knowledge, one would have to ask why people were still daft enough to swim in it? However, this was where the camp was planned for that Saturday night. There were many great places to pitch a tent around the quarry and the lads picked a spot, with short grass, that was perfectly level.

They arrived around five o'clock that afternoon and began pitching the tent which was borrowed from Anto. It was quite large and slept six. Anto was there to show them how to put it together but would not be staying this time because he had to work.

When the tent was up, the sleeping bags stowed away and everything unpacked, Anto left the boys to their own devices. They decided to go for a walk around the area leaving one person behind to guard the site. The person left behind was Shifty, the laziest one. He wouldn't walk the length of himself if he didn't have to.

An hour later they were all back at the camp site and the decision was made to get a fire going and make some tea. This was quite easily accomplished and the kettle was put on to boil. As an extra treat some potatoes were placed in the fire to roast. When the tea was finished, the potatoes peeled, salted and eaten, fingers burnt, sucked and nursed, all the utensils were washed and put away.

Red had brought along his guitar and after some coaxing he started to play and sing the popular songs of the day. The boys joined in and a happy mood descended over the camp. It was now dark and Po lit two Tilley Lamps. They were all seated around the brightly glowing fire when the story telling began.

"Do ya know, dozens of people drowned here?" said Bishop.

"I know, and their bodies were never found," added Shifty.

"How far would the top of the quarry be from the water would ya say Red?" asked Po.

"Don't know, fifty, hundred feet I suppose."

"Ya'd have ta be crazy ta dive in, wouldn't ya?" commented Bishop.

"Well I know I wouldn't do it," stated Red.

"I heard that people, late at night, have seen the spirit of one of the Christian Brothers that was divin' here and drowned."

"Maybe we'll see him tonight!" added Po.

"Ya know, we might," said Red.

"My granddad told me about a man who was drowned here. When he dived in, he slipped and hit his head on the sharp rocks. He was supposed ta have his head totally separated from his body when he hit the water. They say he comes back here every night lookin' for his head," related Po, his voice tailing off into a whisper.

"So he had a bad temper then Po?" asked Red.

"Bad temper?"

"Yeah, bad temper. Lost his head, didn't he?"

This brought a round of laughter.

"Ya might not think it's so funny if ya meet him tonight," added Po, still in a whisper.

"Sure that wouldn't be a problem Po," said Red.

"And why's that?"

"Sure if he has no head, he wouldn't be able ta see us."

This brought another round of laughter. The ghost stories continued for over an hour with every one having at least two or three stories that were definitely, without doubt, positively true, about devils, headless coachmen, hoofed feet, Banshees and so on. Then close to midnight, Po was in the middle of a story when the boys heard a noise that seemed to be coming from behind the tent.

"What was that?" asked Bishop.

"Shush," said Po

There was the noise again, a rustling, like someone moving about, behind the tent.

They all stood up.

"Who's there?" shouted Shifty...no response...again he called out, "Who's there?"

There was silence, then a very low deep throated moan.

This was all that was required to spark the boys into action. Within two minutes all four were halfway down Courtney Hill heading into town. They decided to go to Po's house. His parents were away for the weekend. To let themselves be seen and to explain why they left the camp, might give rise to teasing that could last a long time.

Early the next morning, Red and Shifty set out to get the equipment from the camp site leaving Po and Bishop asleep. They arrived at the site and in record time had everything packed up. What they couldn't carry was hidden to collect later. It was only then that they made the shocking discovery.

They returned to Po's house to find Po and the Bishop up and about.

"Well?" asked Po.

"Well what?"

"Did ya see anythin'?"

Red and Shifty exchanged glances.

"Yeah, we did, it was shockin'."

"What was it?"

"Ya know, I'm not sure I even want ta talk about it, what about you Shifty?"

"I'll never talk about what we saw."

"Red, Jasus Christ, ya have ta tell us," pleaded Bishop.

Again Red and Shifty exchanged glances.

"Whaddya think Shifty? Should I tell them?"

Shifty shrugged his shoulders.

"Ok, but ya better gimme some hot tea Po."

Po raced around and in seconds had a mug of steaming tea in Red's hand.

Red sat back in the armchair and took a deep meaningful breath.

"Well, we arrived at the site. It wasn't quite light yet, so we approached the tent very quietly, ya know, just in case?"

"Yeah, yeah."

"Just as we got ta where we'd all been sittin', we both saw it at the same time. It started ta move slowly towards us, making low funny sounds as if it was tryin' ta communicate."

"Could ya make out anythin' it said?" asked Bishop.

"No, not a word. Both of us were glued to the spot. It was as if we couldn't move."

"Did it keep comin' at ya?" asked Po.

"It did, but very slowly."

"What did it look like?"

"I tell ya, it was bad. I'm not sure you're ready ta hear this, or if I really wanna tell ya."

"Tell us, no matter how bad it was," said Bishop.

"Ok then, well, we could tell it wasn't human."

"I friggin' knew it," whispered Po.

"Shush Po, let him tell the story."

"As I said, we knew both of us, that this thing wasn't human."

"As it got closer I noticed the hoofed feet."

"Jasus," exclaimed Po.

"And the awful horns."

"I friggin' knew it, we shouldn't a gone there, it was the Devil," panted Bishop.

"Ya could be right Bishop. It could a been a devil all right, but it was a devil called Daisy! It was one of Jackie Sands friggin' cows."

End

The Ghost

1960

"Ah, come on Red, they can't be that bad?" pleaded Po, walking backward in front of Red.

"No chance."

"But sure, I'm your best mate, your buddy, your friend, the guy who knows all your secrets, the guy…"

"All right, all right, for Christ sake, ya can come, ok?" Red spat out.

"Brilliant, I knew ya loved me," Po smiled.

"Piss off ya wee rat. I hope it rains on your birthday," grumbled Red. "What time ya goin'?"

"About seven, and I'm not waitin' for ya. If you're not there I'm goin' on, ok?"

"I'll be there, don't worry," replied Po grinning from ear to ear.

Tuesday night was Red's night to visit his girlfriend, Maureen, who lived about five miles from Newry on the road to Rathfriland. She was a tall, elegant girl with long blond hair, stunning blue eyes, and a face and figure of which young men's dreams were made. Red met her at a dance in Newry some six months earlier and had been going out with her since. Po knew Maureen, having met her with Red on a number of occasions.

"I'll never understand the way girls think," Po mused to Red.

"Why would a beautiful girl like Maureen go out with an ugly, lanky, moron like you…amazin'?"

"She has taste."

Red enjoyed keeping Po wound up about Maureen's sisters.

"Maureen's two sisters were at the dance last week. They saw ya talkin' to us and tortured me ta find out about ya. Now they definitely have no taste."

"Do they look like Maureen?" Po would ask earnestly.

"Well, in some ways they do," was Red's standard answer.

"Holy shit Red, ya have ta fix me up with one of them, ya have ta, no jokin' now."

"I'll think about it, maybe," was the droll reply.

That night as Red cycled through the town on his way to pick up Po, he smiled to himself thinking of Po with Maureen's two sisters. 'They'll eat him alive' he thought as a grin spread across his face.

Po was sitting on his bike ready and waiting. His hair flattened with Brylcreem, he was dressed in his new white Mac, tied casually around the waist like some movie star. Red slapped him on the back of the head.

"What was that for?"

"Nothin', wait till ya do somethin'," Red raced ahead leaving Po rubbing his head.

They chatted on the way, although, to be honest, it was Po who did most of the talking. He must have asked Red twenty questions before they got two miles out of Newry.

"Which one'll I go for Red?"

"Which one do ya think is the best lookin'?"

"What are their names?"

"Are they tall?"

Red just grunted most of his answers. They finally arrived at Maureen's house. Her parents, as luck would have it, had gone to visit a sick relative and it was Maureen who opened the door.

"Hi Red."

She smiled and kissed Red on the cheek, then noticed Po. "Hi Po, what a nice surprise," She bent forward and kissed Po on the cheek. Po

looked down at his shuffling feet not wanting Red to see him blush. Red was staring at him. Po kicked him on the ankle, "Shut up you."
"I never opened ma mouth," laughed Red rubbing his ankle.
"Well, don't," snarled Po.

They followed Maureen into the sitting room where Ann, the youngest sister was standing. She said hello to Red and then looked at Po.
"Ann, this is Po," said Maureen before turning to the fireside chair where her other sister sat, "and this is Marie."
Po glanced at Red. No words were spoken, but Red knew exactly what Po was silently saying to him. 'You're one dead bastard Morgan. I will get ya for this if it takes forever.'
Red had somehow forgotten to mention that Ann was ten years old and her big sister, Marie, was looking forward to her twelfth birthday next week.

After some tea and biscuits, Red and Maureen decided to go for a walk. Po would be entertained by the two sisters who were now giggling and whispering to one another.

Two hours later Red and Maureen returned to find Po and the girls sitting on the floor playing cards. They all had more tea and biscuits and chatted for some time before Red noticed that it was after eleven o'clock.
"Time we were hittin' the road Maureen," said Red as he stood.
"Ok, will you be out on Thursday?" asked Maureen.
"For sure," answered Red.
After the goodbyes, Po discovered to his dismay, that he had a puncture in the front wheel of his bicycle.
"What'll I do now, I have no repair kit with me," moaned Po.
"Just leave the bike here, we can organise to get it tomorrow," said Red, inspecting the wheel.
"You can hop on the bar of mine for now and when we see a car; ya can get off and hitch, ok?"
"Sounds good ta me," smiled Po. The boys set off towards Newry.
Red wasn't worried about having Po on the bar of his bike as two thirds of the way home was downhill. After ten minutes on the road they heard a car coming behind them. Po jumped off the bike and began

hitching. The car stopped and Po shouted over his shoulder as he ran to the car.

"See ya tomorrow." He got in and was gone before Red even reached the spot where the car stopped. Red smiled to himself as he remembered the abuse he got from Po when they left Maureen's house.

"You are one downright sneaky, lying, two-faced, not-to-be-trusted bastard."

"Sure I love ya too Po," smiled Red.

"Why didn't ya tell me what age they were?"

"Ya didn't ask!"

"Shit!"

"Now Po, ya had a good night, didn't ya?" pointed out Red.

"That doesn't matter, so I had a good night, that doesn't change the fact that ya set me up, ya scumbag."

Red just laughed.

"You're dead Morgan, some night I'm gonna sneak into your house and do ya when you're sleepin'."

"Po, I never knew I turned ya on like that?"

"Piss off ya bastard."

Red was making good time as he sped down the twisting road towards Newry. The dynamo on his back wheel was whining loudly with the speed giving him a bright, almost white headlight. Suddenly as he rounded a bend a white figure appeared in his headlight. His heart jumped and he braked as hard as he could. The bike wobbled and skidded and eventually ended up in the ditch. Red picked himself up and was feeling a nasty knock on his left leg when he heard a familiar voice.

"Ya all right Red?" it was Po!

"What?" Red was still confused. "What the hell are ya doing here ya wee bastard?"

"Ah, did you have a wee accident Red?" smirked Po.

"I'll wee accident ya when I get my hands on ya," growled Red.

Po was now sitting on the grass, roaring with laughter.

"It's not that funny ya ejit," complained Red.

Po didn't hear beyond his own laughter.

"What? What's so funny, tell me?"

"Ya won't believe it Red, ya just won't believe it," panted Po.

"What, what won't I believe?"

"Well ta start with, whaddya think of that?" giggled Po pointing to something in the ditch a few yards away.

Red moved a little closer to see where Po was pointing.

"A bike?"

"A bike," laughed Po.

"Who owns it?" asked Red.

"Well now, that's the story. About five minutes ago I saw this light comin' down the hill," said Po, trying his best to tell the story.

"I thought it was you."

".….and?"

"Well, I thought I would get my own back on ya, so I hid in the ditch and waited," Po had to stop to get his breath.

"When it was almost here, I jumped out waving my arms and goin' woooo," laughed Po demonstrating the whole action for Red.

"It was some auld farmer and he nearly shit!" panted Po.

"He jumped off the bike and ran off down that side road like the clappers."

Red was now doubled himself.

"All he saw in the light was ma white coat," laughed Po.

When the two had settled down, Po got on the farmer's bike and they both peddled off towards Newry. Po left the bike outside the Police Station later that night.

"That auld farmer, he will be telling all his mates in the Pub how he saw a ghost on the Rathfriland Road," laughed Po as they arrived outside his house.

"And getting plenty of pints bought for him as well. He will get years out of that story," returned Red, heading off up the street waving back to Po.

End

The Record Hop

1960

"No."
"But Red?" pleaded Po.
"No."
"She's not bad ya know."
"No."
"Listen, will ya? It's only for one night."
"No."
"She has a good body."
"No."
"Plus the fact that she fancies ya."
"No."
"Right."
"Right what?"
"So, ya'll think about it then?"
"No."
"I knew ya would."
"No."

Po and Red turned into Uncle Luigi's and slid into the first snug beside Anto who was having his morning break.

"Well, if it isn't Pinkie and Perky."

"What's the craic Anto?"

"Frig all, I'm pissed off."

"What's wrong?" asked Red.

"Friggin' two staff off sick, so I'm stuck here in this friggin' place, all day, and tonight."

"So you're not goin' tonight then?"

"My Record Hop tonight will be the friggin' jukebox."

"Shit," said Red.

"Shit is right," agreed Anto. "Ya gonna chat up your one with the legs tonight then Po?"

"For sure."

"What about her mate and shadow then?"

Po looked at Red.

"No."

"I think I can talk Red into distractin' the shadow."

"No ya can't."

"Red you're his best mate. Ya have ta help your mate in a time of need."

"Oh Jasus, he's got ta you too has he?"

Both Anto and Po burst into laughter together.

"See you, you're a wee weasel Hillen."

Po put his arm around Red's shoulders and started kissing him on the cheek.

"My bestest mate in the whole world," he mumbled between kisses.

Anto stood up, leaned across and tried to kiss the other cheek.

"Ach sure he is Po, and a lovely wee fella as well."

Red stood up brushing off Anto and Po.

"Will ya get off ya two fruits."

He sat down again to the laughter of his two companions. Red held up both palms facing Po.

"Look, this is as far as I'll go, right? I'll chat ta your one for a bit ta let ya have time with legs eleven, ok? That's all! I'm not takin' her home, no way, not tonight, not any night, not ever, right?"

"Isn't he a great guy?" said Po to a grinning Anto.

"Ah Jasus Red, come over ta I give ya a kiss," said Anto.

"You can piss off too, fruit."

Later that night, decked out in their Sunday best, Red and Po climbed the steps to the entrance of The Bucket.

"Now ya remember, I'm only gonna talk ta your one for a while, ok?"

"Yes Red," said Po sweetly.

"Dick," murmured Red.

"That makes ya a dick's mate then," came back Po. This got him a punch on the arm that made him wince. Once inside, the sounds of Bill Haley and the Comets had the already packed hall on the floor dancing. The boys made their way with some difficulty to the far corner of the room where the rest of their mates usually could be found. Red recognised a few faces as he finally found a seat on the window sill, squeezing in beside Dunno McManus.

"Red, look at your one in the blue dress," said Dunno nodding in the direction of the dance floor.

"Not bad," said Red.

"Not bad? Are ya crazy? She's the sexiest thing in here," stated Dunno. "She's what wet dreams are made of."

"Dunno, you'd have a wet dream over a duck," was Red's answer.

"Frig off."

Red just shook his head.

"Hey, Red, she's here." Red looked up and saw Po emerging from the crowd on the dance floor.

"I saw her over by the Snack Bar."

"And…?"

"What?"

"What are ya tellin' me for? Why don't ya go and ask her ta dance then?"

"Do ya think I should?"

"Jasus," Red turned Po around by the shoulders and gave him a push in the back that landed him well out onto the dance floor.

"Yo Red," shouted an approaching Anto.

"I thought ya were workin'?"

"Got a stand in."

"Where's Po?"

"I think he's over there, gettin' up the nerve ta ask your one ta dance."

"Will he get out with her?"

"She'll probably go out with him ta stop him talkin'."

An hour later Red was getting an orange drink when Po arrived beside him.

"Well," greeted Po.

"Did ya dance her?"

"Three times."

"Jasus, you're a real Don Juan."

"I'm gettin' her a drink."

"So, you're movin' in are ya?"

"Well, I haven't asked her out yet, I'm waitin' on the right moment." Red looked around.

"Well, I wouldn't wait too long if I were you. There's another guy snoggin' her on the floor."

Po spun around.

"Where?"

The colour had left his face.

"Gotcha," laughed Red.

"Whorin' bastard," Po snarled.

"Po, and you an Altar Boy. I'm so ashamed of ya."

Po stuck two fingers up in front of Red's face and disappeared into the crowd with his two bottles of orange. Red got up and danced a few times with girls he knew and was in fact, having a good time.

"Red, Red?" came Po's voice.

"What?"

"Come on."

"Come on where?"

"I need ya ta chat ta your one now, come on will ya?" Po urged.

Red turned to Anto who was sitting beside him.

"The sacrifices one has ta make," said Red rubbing a hand across his forehead. He didn't get to hear the answer because he was being dragged across the floor.

They arrived at the table where Po's girl and her friend were seated.

"Noreen, this is Red," Red shook hands with her.

"And this is Josie," Red shook hands with Josie.

There were two empty chairs, one beside each of the girls. Red immediately went for the chair beside Noreen, but he never made it. Two hands grabbed him and redirected him to the chair beside Josie.

"Thanks for your help Po."

"Don't mention it."

Red no sooner sat down when Po and Noreen were making their way onto the dance floor.

"So, hello again Red. I like your jacket. Po told me a lot about ya."

"Po tells lies ya know."

Josie made a loud sort of snort that was meant to be a laugh.

"Have ya a girlfriend Red?" said Josie around her gum chewing.

"No, not at the moment."

'Shit, I'm one dumb, stupid bastard with a giant mouth,' he thought.

"Really?" Josie moved closer.

"Can't hear ya way over there with the noise."

Her perfume filled Red's head. He had to make an effort not to smile when he thought, 'It's called, 'Moonlight at the Dump' a shillin' a barrel'.

Josie told Red about her mom, her sisters, especially the one who borrowed her clothes all the time without asking, her last boyfriend, his bad habits, her likes, her dislikes, her dreams for the future…

Red looked at his watch, 'Christ' he thought, 'They're only gone ten minutes!'

He caught Anto's eye as he was passing on the way to the toilets. The smile said it all. 'There's a bastard; he and that wee rat planned this.'

"Would you excuse me a minute, going to the Gents," Red said.

"Sure, do one for me," she snorted again.

Red came up beside Anto at the urinal.

"See you, you're a bastard."

"What did I do?" smiled Anto.

"That friggin' woman is puttin' me into a coma."

"That bad, huh?"

"That bad."

"Ya know her, don't ya?"

"Well, I sorta know her."

"Ya sorta know her? Ya know what she's like all right ya bastard," snapped Red.

"Ah, but sure poor Po, he's mad about your one."

"No, nearly right. He's just friggin' mad."

"Well, sure when ya leave her home just don't ask her out again."

"Leave her home, now I know you're havin' a laugh."

"Red, now I want ya to stay very calm now, ok?"

"Are you gonna say somethin' I'm not gonna like Anto?"

"Well, sort of, maybe."

"Tell me."

Anto was trying harder than he had ever tried before…not to laugh. He failed miserably. He fell against the toilet wall and just let go. He thought his sides were going to rip apart. Red just stared at him.

"Come on, tell me ya bastard."

Anto squeezed out a few words.

"Po…Po's gone…home."

"He's what?"

"Gone…left…departed," roared Anto.

"With your one?"

"Yeah."

"And this one?" Red pointed a thumb in the direction of the hall.

"They told her…" Anto had to bend over.

"For frigs sake, told her what?"

"Told her…" Anto straightened up and took a deep breath.

"Ya were takin' her home, and she was friggin' delighted," Anto was away again, bent in two with tears running down his face.

"I'll kill him, I will, I'll kill him, as sure as God, I'll friggin' break his scrawny wee neck."

This did not in any way help Anto, if anything it made him worse. He slid down the wall and was now on the floor.

"I swear ta God, that wee rat is dead meat. I will, I swear it, I'll kill him."

"Ya better go Red, your girlfriend is waitin' on ya," sobbed Anto.

Red left the toilets using a long catalogue of obscenities about both Po and Anto, their parents, and their ancestors. He actually did leave Josie home and she did actually stop talking, twice, the first time to change her gum and the second to kiss Red goodnight.

On the way home Red's mind was racing. He passed the time thinking of the slowest and most painful way he could kill Po. Nothing he thought of even came close.

Po had a great night!

End

God's Pub

1960

Red Morgan turned the key in the large oak door and beckoned to the three shadowy figures crouched behind a tree at the side of Newry Cathedral. The three, still crouching, reached Red as he opened the door to the vestry. Silently they slipped inside and Red closed the door behind them. Someone giggled.

"Shush for frig sake," whispered Red. "Follow me, and remember, no noise."

He produced a tiny pencil torch from his pocket giving them just enough light. The intruders reached the door and went through.

"Now mind where you're walkin'…there are stairs."

Slowly they descended the twelve steps to the church basement and followed Red into a large room. Red closed the door and switched on the light.

"Well, here we are," said Po to Dunno and Jumpy.

"Jasus, this is some place," whispered Dunno.

"It's ok in here Dunno, no need ta whisper. We could have a singsong and no one would hear us down here."

Red produced four plastic glasses from his pocket and reached inside one of the many cardboard boxes stacked against the wall. He took out a bottle of red wine.

"Po, give us the needle," said Red, hand outstretched towards Po.

Po reached into his pocket. He produced a metal syringe and needle 'borrowed' from his diabetic aunt.

"I hope you washed this Po?" said Red.

"Friggin' sure. I actually boiled it."

Red handed one of the glasses to Po. He just nodded and went to the sink at the other end of the room where he filled the glass with water. Red inserted the needle through the cork of the bottle and filled the syringe with wine which he released into one of the glasses. He then put the needle into the glass of water and filled the syringe again. The needle was carefully reinserted through the same hole and topped the bottle up with the water. He repeated this procedure many times until he had four glasses of wine. Red raised his glass in the air.

"Here's ta your first visit."

The conspirators took a large drink of their wine.

"Jasus that stuffs rotten," complained Jumpy.

"That's the very best of French wine I'll have ya know. De ya think the priests here'd drink auld cheap stuff?" said Red.

"He's right lads. This is expensive wine, ya wouldn't believe what this stuff costs."

Three glasses later, everyone was beginning to feel the effects of the wine.

"Be Jasus you're right Red. This is some quare stuff," said Dunno.

"I'll drink to that," slurred Jumpy.

Po had left moments before to visit the toilets. He returned slowly through the door and spoke in a deep voice.

"Now my children let us give thanks."

He was dressed in a priest's cassock and surplus. All three stared open mouthed before breaking into fits of laughter. Po was enjoying himself.

"Now my children, we are gathered here at this time to sip from what the good Lord has kindly provided. Let us give thanks."

All glasses were lifted in the air and a toast was made.

"Here's to what the good Lord has provided."

There was some singing, some dancing, some stories, even some discussion and arguments about football before Red looked at his watch.

"We have to go now lads, sure it's gone half past twelve."

"No way, it couldn't be," said Po.

He checked his watch.

"Shit it is."

It took a few minutes to tidy the room. With warnings from Red to be quiet, the giggling lads left the cathedral. While the three boys waited in a doorway, Red crossed the street to the priest's house, unlocked the door and entered. A minute later, having returned the keys he'd kept after evening Mass, he was back outside. They all made their way along Hill Street, singing a chorus of every song they could remember.

Next morning Po arrived at Red's house in Castle Street. He found Red sitting outside on the footpath.

"What are ya doin' out here?" Po asked.

"Granda's cooking."

"Oh shit, tripe?"

"Yeah."

"Jasus, I can smell it. How do people eat that stuff?"

Red stood up. "Come on, let's go down the town."

"Before I forget," Po punched Red hard on the arm.

"You are a bastard and a frigger and a whore so ya are."

"What the hell did I do?" asked Red rubbing his arm.

"I could have got hammered last night. When I went in, me ma and da were still up."

"So what the hell has that to do with me?"

"Ya know damn well what ya did, or should a say, what ya didn't do! I'm talkin' about last night. Ya let me walk home and into my kitchen to face me ma and da, wearing a friggin' priests collar!"

"Jasus no."

"Jasus yes."

Red burst out laughing.

"It's not funny, bastard."

That didn't help Red any.

"Ya know what my ma's like. She does the flowers on the Altar and all that stuff."

"I know," Red managed to get out.

"Good job I hang around with you, bastard."

"Why?"

"I've learned to lie at the drop of a hat."

"What did ya say?"

"I told them I was practicin' for a play we're doin' ta raise money for charity."

"Jasus, you're good. No doubt about it."

"Well, that's not the point, ya should'a told me about the stupid collar."

"I never even noticed it, I swear."

"Yeah, I believe ya."

"Seriously, I never even noticed it. But, hi, we did have a good night's craic, didn't we?"

"We sure did."

They entered Uncle Luigi's Café, got two Cokes and sat down. They were shortly joined by Bishop Keenan and Topcoat Anderson.

"Where were you guys last night?"

"Out havin' a great time," said Red.

Red and Po clinked their bottles together.

"Where'd ya go?" asked The Bishop.

"Ah now, we were at a very secret place with dancin' and singin' and loads a free drink."

"Yeah, pull the other one," said Topcoat.

Po looked at Red.

"Am I tellin' lies?"

"Every word is the truth, for sure."

"So, where's this place," asked Topcoat.

"It's a pub we go ta sometimes," said Po with a cheeky grin across his face.

"What's it called?" asked The Bishop.

"Should I tell them?" Po asked Red.

"Why not."

"It's the best pub in Newry and they're very careful who they let in, very selective so they are."

"So what's it called?" asked Topcoat.

Red and Po looked at each other, clinked bottles again, both making the toast in one voice.

"God's Pub!"

End

The Spud Pickers

1960

"You're one lazy bastard," complained Po to Red.

"It's ten past seven. We should've been there before seven."

"Get stuffed," mumbled Red. "I should still be in my friggin' bed."

"You agreed last night we needed the money for the weekend, lazy bastard."

"Yeah, yeah, yeah, I'm here aren't I, so stop naggin' me. You're worse than an auld doll."

A short time later Po and Red arrived at the Stone Bridge. It was a beautiful morning with a clear blue sky…not that Red noticed. Last night he was at the Parochial Hall and refused to leave early with Po. The Miami Showband was playing and Red had 'clicked' with a somewhat well proportioned young lady from Hilltown. He stayed with her until the end of the night and then some. It was after three in the morning when he got home. He was regretting that now.

There were six others standing at the Stone Bridge. This was the meeting point where farmers arrived in the mornings to take on extra help for the day. At this time of year the crop was potatoes.

"Mornin' Red," came the bright welcome from Shifty. "A wee late night, had we?"

"Get stuffed," was all the reply he got. This of course caused a round of sniggers.

"Anybody come yet?" asked Po.

"Naw, nothin' yet," replied Shifty.

"Hi Red, I heard ya clicked last night," said Shifty turning his attention to Red again.

"Is that what ya heard?"

"Well?"

"Well what?"

"Well how did it go?"

"Top band, the Miami."

"No, I mean the bird."

"Great sound."

"What?"

"Definitely brilliant."

Po was enjoying this. Long hard experience had taught him what Red was like. Getting information out of him was like trying to open a tin can with a lollipop stick.

"She was good, huh?"

"Very tight, made the hairs stand up on the back of my neck at times."

"Jasus!"

"Oh yeah, unbelievable!"

"Where did ya go?"

"Right up the front."

"Jasus, she really wanted it huh?"

"Who?"

"Your one, ya know?"

"No I don't know. I'm talking about the band, what are you talkin' about?"

"Oh, frig off Red."

Red turned to Po, his arms outstretched.

"What did I do now?"

"Nothin', not a thing, nothin' a'tall, not one single thing," answered Po, shaking his head.

"And frig you too Hillen."

Po looked at Red.

"Isn't that just lovely? The language ya have ta listen ta."

"Personally I think it's a disgrace, the town's goin' downhill," replied Red with a straight face.

"That's it Red, ya hit the nail on the head…downhill…that's where it's goin'."

Just then the sound of a horn halted the conversation. Red looked up as the lorry pulled up beside them. The driver, an unshaven farmer in his middle sixties, stuck his bald head out the window.

"Mornin' lads, what ya lookin?"

Lanky spoke up first, "Fifteen bob."

"Who's your man? Fifteen bob, aye right. Seven bob and dinner, who's for it?"

Po spoke up, "Tell ya what, twelve bob and ya got the best team in the town."

"Ah Jasus now lads, do ya think I'm made a money? Look, I'll tell ya what I'll do, and I'm goin' right over the top here," he rubbed his stubbled chin and gave a toothless grin.

"Ten bob and we're in business."

Po looked around at everyone and then back at the farmer.

"Done."

"Right, get aboard me lads; yis'll have me and me poor wife and childer in the poor house."

Some twenty minutes later the lorry pulled into a field close to Mayobridge. Waiting there was another man leaning against the wheel of a tractor.

"Where did ya get this lot? They don't look like there's a day's work between them."

"Ah now," answered the first farmer getting out of his truck. "Sure that's all there was and didn't they stick me for ten bob."

"What? Jasus Christ, man, are ya outta your skull…ten bob?" He turned to look at the lads standing at the lorry.

"Now lads, a joke's a joke, ten bob? Sure you'll all take eight so as we can break even on the auld spuds?"

"Ya know, you're right," spoke up Po "Ten bob, I don't know what we were thinkin'. Give me your hand and we'll settle on twelve."
The two farmers looked at each other and burst into laughter.
"Get away on with yis now and get them praties lifted."

This was a regular routine between the farmers and the pickers. They both knew the money agreed in Newry was what would be paid. The banter was just a bit of fun to get the day started. The tractor started up and began beating and spreading the drills. The boys began the work of picking the potatoes and putting them in baskets which, when full, would be emptied at selected areas in the field to be picked up later by the tractor.

Red stopped for a moment, stretched his back, and looked up at the clear blue summer sky. It was getting hot now as lunchtime approached. Po, who was working beside him also stopped and, shading his eyes, looked up to the sky.
"Gettin' to be a friggin' scorcher, huh?"
"If it was cold or rainin' you'd still be complainin'," snarled Red.
"Ah shut up grumpy, wonder what's for dinner?"
"Well, it's always been good here and plenty of it," replied Red.
Just then, as if on cue, they heard the farmer shouting.
"Grub's up lads."
They all made their way to the farmhouse. As they neared the two storey white building the smell of cooking met their nostrils and somehow seemed to quicken their step. Outside the back door they all removed their boots and entered the farm kitchen where they were embraced in the warmth of culinary aromas that only a farm kitchen can muster. The farmer's wife, a stout grey haired lady, turned from her chores at the large black stove and smiled broadly as she faced the workers,
"Sit where ya like boys," she said pointing to the huge wooden table that commanded the middle of the large kitchen. A number of serving bowls were filled to capacity with boiled potatoes, cabbage, and turnips. The plates were soon piled with fried back bacon and they were told there was plenty more. There were also large plates of home baked bread, still warm from the oven. After all the trouser belts were loosened, and everyone was on their second mug of tea, their third or

fourth thick slice of buttered bread and their second Woodbine, they got the 'hurry up' shouts from the farmer.

The afternoon passed quickly and it was getting close to quitting time. At the corner of the field, the second tractor had started loading the picked potatoes into a very high metal-sided trailer. The pickers made their way to the tractors and were throwing in any loose potatoes that had fallen out during the loading. When the trailer was filled three feet above its sides Red turned to Po.
"Where's Shifty? He has my matches."
They looked around but Shifty could not be seen.
"Hi, did any of you guys see Shifty?" shouted Red.
"Is that the curly haired guy?" asked the tractor driver.
"Yeah, that's him," answered Red.
"Last time I saw him he was brushin' out the trailer."
Red and Po swapped glances.
"Naw, he wouldn't be that stupid."
"Hang on," said Red.
"Shifty!" he shouted. No one answered.
"Christ, he's under the spuds," murmured Po very quietly.
"What?" shouted the farmer, "He's in the trailer?"
"Well, he's not here, and that's the last place he was seen," said Red.
"Jasus Christ," shouted the farmer as he ran towards the tractor. He pulled a leaver and started revving the engine and the trailer started to tip. The other farmer had released the bars on the back of the trailer and the spuds started to spill out onto the ground.
"You lot, start spreading them spuds in case he is under them," shouted the second farmer. Everyone worked without a word. There was a sense of urgency in their movements. A few minutes later a voice behind Red asked, "What ya looking for?" Red turned around and there stood Shifty with a one inch long Woodbine held between his lips.
"What the shit?" panted Red. "Where were ya?"
"In the next field having a piss, why?"

By the time Shifty had sprinted to the far end of the field he must have been hit by at least twenty spuds, some of which were thrown by the farmers.

All the way home Shifty complained,
"Can't even have a piss without bein' battered."
This of course just got him more slaps on the head.
Such is the hard, unfair life of a Spud Picker.

The New Suit

1960

"Red ya have ta come with me," pleaded Po.

Red looked across the table at Po.

"Look, I don't want ta get involved in this, your ma will get ya a nice suit."

"Will she hell. I'll end up with some stupid thing a farmer wouldn't wear."

"Sure what could I do? If your ma decides on a suit I can't tell her not ta get it for ya."

"She'll listen ta you so she will."

"If I go with ya, you'll owe me, right?"

"I'll owe ya big time."

"Big time?"

"Big time."

"All right then, I'll go."

"Ah sure you've been a really good mate ta me over the years…once or twice."

Red took a swing at Po who dodged it expertly.

Later that day Red was standing outside Turkington's men's shop on Hill Street. He didn't have to wait long, Po and his mom had just turned the corner. She had her finger waving in his face. Red grinned, 'Poor Po, he's gettin' it for somethin',' he thought.

"Hi Red," said Po.

"Red will ya tell this fella he's too young ta be wearin' a three piece suit. I think he thinks he's a film star or somethin'."

"You're far two young ta be wearin' a three piece suit Po. De ya think you're a film star or what?" said Red into Po's face.

Po mimed the word 'Shithead' perfectly.

All three entered the shop. After twenty minutes of looking at about ten suits which Po hated, his mom was beginning to get impatient.

"That green suit is lovely, it suits your colouring so it does, doesn't it Red?" stated Po's mom.

"Not too bad a'tall that one."

If looks could kill, Red would now be in a coffin.

"Ma, are ya crazy, a green suit? No way!"

"Look I haven't all day ta be standin' here with ya. Now you'll settle for one of these suits and that's that."

"Which one do ya like the best?" Red whispered to Po when he got the chance.

"I suppose the blue one's not bad, but I wanted a three piece."

"Just shut up and take that one, I'll sort it."

Red went to the counter where Philip Doran was doing some paperwork.

"Hi ya Phil."

"Red, long time no see. How's yourself?"

"Strugglin' bravely. How much is that blue suit Po was lookin' at?"

"The blue one…ah, that's twenty one pounds."

"And how much to make a waistcoat ta match it?"

"Same material…I suppose we could do it for five pounds."

"Ok, ya have a deal, now ya'll have ta play along, ok?"

"I suppose," laughed Philip.

"Loan me your pen."

Red went back to Po and his mom.

"Ya know, ya might be right about that green one Mrs. Hillen, let's look at it again."

"See…see, at least Red's got some taste," said Mrs. Hillen, finger stabbing Po in the chest. She left them to get the green suit.

"Are ya friggin' out of your friggin' skull Morgan? I wouldn't be seen dead in that thing."

"Look, just play along for the moment will ya?"

Po nodded. The green suit arrived. Red moved away to the suit rack. When he returned he was carrying the blue suit.

"Naw, havin' seen it again, I don't think it suits him. Anyway, it's too light for him, ya have to have it in the cleaners every other day, ya know what he's like," said Red giving Po's mom a knowing look.

"Ya could be right there Red, he is a scruffy wee bugger."

"Now, this dark blue is just the job."

"You're right Red, that will do him perfectly."

Po got a slap across the back of the head.

"Why can't ya be sensible like your friend Red just for once?"

Mrs. Hillen and the two boys left the shop after paying for the suit and having it wrapped. The two boys said goodbye to Mrs. Hillen at the corner and walked off down Hill Street.

"I thought ya were supposed ta help ya frigger…some help!"

"Ah but Po, I did help, I got ya your three piece suit."

"What? You're talkin' shit."

"I had a chat with Phil Doran and he is gettin' ya a waistcoat made for that suit."

"How the frig did ya manage that?"

"It was simple, the suit cost twenty one pounds, the waistcoat, five pounds. So, I changed the price tag on the suit to read twenty six pounds…see? Now your waistcoat's paid for and it will be ready next Thursday."

"Ya devious bastard."

"What can I say?" said Red smugly.

"That deserves a Coke."

"Coke shit, I want a chip as well. Devious bastards don't come cheap ya know!"

End

Bird Catching

1960

It was a sunny Saturday morning in July as Red, and Po with Red's Uncle Pajoe McArdle and his mate John McAllister walked into a field at Ballyholland. Both Red and Po liked these bird catching trips into the countryside. The idea of taking part in an illegal action with adults and being condoned by them had a special appeal for the boys.

Birds were Pajoe's life. He spent every minute he could in the top room of his house where he kept his aviary. There was quite a colourful collection of canaries, budgies and the wild birds finches and greys. These birds were well known and appreciated for their singing. Today's outing was to get some new finches. Pajoe had orders for five which he sold for three shillings each.

Earlier that morning Red and Po helped Pajoe get his equipment ready. There were dozens of twelve inch straight twigs that had been three quarters covered in black sticky roofing pitch; three inches was left clean for handling. These twigs were kept in a plastic tube. Next there was the caller, a hen finch, placed in a tiny eight inch square cage. Pajoe made these cages himself. There was also a twelve inch piece of coarse burlap tacked to a round piece of wood and tied at the top with cord. This was called a holding bag. Lastly was a bottle of methylated spirit.

After searching out a good set, Pajoe decided on a small bush in the middle of the field. The caller's cage was placed down into the centre of the bush. The pitch covered twigs were then slit at the clean ends and slipped over as many of the outer branches as possible. They found a hiding place behind a hedge about ten yards away and sat down to wait.

It didn't take long for the caller to spot some finches and begin singing. After circling a few times a finch swooped down and landed on one of the pitch covered twigs. It was immediately trapped. Everyone raced to the bush and Pajoe gently took hold of the bird. He removed the twig, cleaned its feet, wings and body for pitch residue. The bird was then put in the holding bag and they all returned to their hiding place. This procedure was repeated until Pajoe had his five finches.

It was just before the fifth bird landed that Po asked Pajoe if he could retrieve it and permission was granted.
"You retrieve a bird? Are ya sure ya know which bush ta go ta?" laughed Red.
"I can do it, no problem. I'm a professional bird catcher ya know."
"Po, go bite yourself," said Red giving him the finger.
"Po, one's down, go!" said Pajoe.
Po raced toward the set, turning around to shout at Red.
"And it's Super Po, bird catcher extraordinaire."
Unfortunately he didn't notice the piece of granite sticking out of the ground. He hit it with his foot and it propelled him forward head first into the set.

When the other three arrived Po was totally covered with pitch trying to extradite himself from the set. Expletives were plentiful. The fact that his three companions were in fits of laughter didn't help.
"Po, just ease yourself out slowly," said John, trying to sound concerned.
"I'm friggin' tryin' so I am," snarled Po.
"Keep your hands away from your face Po," said Pajoe.

"And your mouth," added Red.

The landed bird was retrieved, cleaned and bagged, but Po was not so lucky. There wasn't enough methylated spirit to clean him. He had to walk all the way home covered in sticky black pitch. Throughout the long journey he was quietly praying that God would strike his three companions dumb. His prayers were not answered.

"So, whaddya think the newspaper headlines will read Pajoe?"

"Super Po gets into sticky situation?"

"No, Super Po flies into bush to save bird!"

"Super Po sticks to his guns."

"Big black-out in Ballyholland."

"Flying schoolboy seen in field."

"Is Super Po in debt? No way, he's in the black."

"You've heard of Pitch and Toss? Today we had Toss and Pitch!"

This was the longest two and a half miles Po ever walked!

End

The Strawberry Fields

1960

Red and Po arrived at the Stone Bridge just before eight. There were perhaps twenty people waiting for the lorry from Donaghan's Strawberries. The boys liked picking strawberries, not just for the money, but there was always a good day's craic with the women who worked alongside them as a bonus. Strawberry picking was a popular way to raise cash during the school holidays.

"Well if it isn't himself and himself," Red and Po were greeted by Jammy.
"Hi Jammy, what's happenin'? " replied Po.
"Frig all, nobody's arrived yet. The lorry's usually here at eight."
"Hi Red," chipped in Lanky.
"Lanky, I thought ya were dead. I haven't seen ya in ages."
"Was down in Dublin staying with my Aunty Mary."
"Lucky bastard. All my relatives live in friggin' Newry. You and Po are really lucky," said Red.
"Why am I lucky?" inquired a puzzled Po.
"What I was saying ta Lanky, all my relatives live in Newry whereas you and Lanky…"
"What are ya ravin' about now Morgan?"

"Well you've got relatives all over the place, St.Luke's Asylum in Armagh, Purtysburn Asylum in Belfast, St Andrews…"

Red moved quickly to avoid Po's kick.

"Whore."

"Now, now Po, language."

"Hi Po…Red," came the voice of Kathleen McArdle.

"Hi Kathleen," answered Po.

"Hi Kathleen," mimicked Red.

"Don't mind him Kathleen. He's mad jealous cause ya fancy me and not him."

"Po Hillen, behave yourself," Kathleen smiled, shyly.

"She's right Po Hillen," Red slapped the back of Po's head. "Behave yourself."

"Jasus Morgan, you've no sense a'tall. You're dicin' with death here and ya can't see it," warned Po taking up a fighting stance.

"Here's the lorry," someone shouted.

There was a flurry of movement as the lorry pulled in. With everyone on board, the five mile journey to Donaghan's, just outside Rathfriland, began. Some fifteen minutes later they had arrived and found the familiar face of Bob waiting. Bob was a tall thin man who was always smiling. The fact that he had no teeth made his smile almost comical. He led them into the field to be worked that day.

After being assigned rows…collecting their punnets…they began work. The pickers were paid by the punnet. They usually filled a dozen at a time before carrying them to the top of the field where Bob weighed them and paid cash.

"Hi Red, that Kathleen's a bit of all right, isn't she?"

"Yeah, she's pretty all right."

"Do ya think I have a chance there?"

"Definitely, she has a fancy for ya... plain ta see."

"Ya think so?"

"Well, it's obvious she has no taste, ya'll be in there all right."

"Ach Red, seriously, should I ask her out?"

"Naw, get a gun and shoot her."

"Ach, will ya be friggin' serious for a minute?"

"Po, are ya gonna torture me all day about friggin' Kathleen McArdle?"

"I'm gonna chat her up at lunchtime."

"Good, thank God. So if she says no, ya'll be moanin' in my ear the rest a the day."

"Well, ya said I was in with a good chance."

"Ok, go for it then."

"I will."

"Brilliant."

"Great."

Lunchtime arrived and Po sought out Kathleen. They began talking and laughing. Red saw them walking toward a little glade on the other side of the road where some of the pickers were having lunch. Bob blew his whistle at two o'clock and the workers returned to their places in the field. Po arrived beaming.

"Well?" asked Red.

"Well what?"

"Did ya friggin' ask her out or what?"

"Yeah…I did."

"And…?"

"She said yeah."

"There ya go, I told ya she had no sense."

"Ah…I'm in love."

"Holy Jasus…will ya get a grip ya ejit."

"But she's lovely so she is."

"To you…anythin' in knickers is lovely."

"I got a kiss too."

"It gets worse."

"She has really soft lips."

"Oh…Jasus."

The afternoon dragged for Red who had to listen to Po's ravings about Kathleen non stop. They finished at five and were home in Newry, sitting in Uncle Luigi's drinking Coke at five-thirty.

"What's the craic?" said Anto sitting down beside the boys.

"Don't ask, take my advice, Po will only tell ya."

"What's this?"

"He's in love."

"With who?"

"An angel," butted in Po.

Red and Anto swapped glances and both chose the same spot on the ceiling at which to stare.

"Anto, she's a beauty."

"Who is she?"

"Kathleen McArdle."

"From the Meadow?"

"Yeah."

"Not bad…pity about the brothers though."

"What about them?"

"Two of them… built like tanks. I remember last year they put some guy in hospital for keepin' Kathleen out late."

"Piss off."

"True, ya need ta be careful there."

Po's face took on a worried expression.

Next day, Po and Red were back at Donaghan's. Halfway through the morning, Po was getting ready to take punnets across to Bob. He stopped and looked at Red.

"Does she really have two big brothers?"

"Jasus, are ya goin' back to the Kathleen saga again?"

"Just wonderin'."

"What's wrong wee lover, the big brothers scare ya off?"

"No way, they don't bother me."

"Course not."

"They friggin' don't."

Lunch time came and Po went looking for Kathleen. Red was sitting with Jammy and Lanky when Kathleen ran up to them.

"Red…can ya come over ta the woods, Po's had an accident," she panted.

Red and the other two boys hurried into the woods where they found Po, in obvious pain, sitting against a tree.

"Po…what happened?" asked Red as he knelt down.

"Jasus."

"Tell me, what happened?"

"I'm in friggin' agony."

"What happened?"

"It's friggin' caught so it is."

"What's caught?"

"My friggin' dick's caught."

"Your dick's caught?"

"In the friggin' zipper."

"Oh Christ, show me?"

Red inspected the snagged appendage.

"Have any a yis got a knife?"

"I've a penknife... here," said Jammy, handing it to Red.

"Hi, hold on a friggin' minute, what are ya gonna do with that knife?"

"There's nothin' else for it, Po. I'm gonna have ta cut it off."

"Are ya frig! No way, piss off. You're not cuttin' my thing off."

"Not your thing ya moron, the zipper."

"Oh…right…go on then for frigs sake."

Red proceeded to cut the zipper and set Po free. Po breathed a deep sigh of relief.

"Jasus, that was sore."

"What were ya doin' ya ejit?"

"I was just havin' a piss and got it caught when I pulled up the zipper."

"Are ya sure it was a piss ya were havin?" smirked Lanky.

"Die Lanky, just die," spat back Po.

That evening Red, Po and some of the gang were sitting out the back of Uncle Luigi's chatting to Anto.

"So, wait a minute. You're sayin' Po was tryin' his hand with your one and got his thing caught in the zipper?"

"No I friggin' wasn't, don't listen ta that frigger Red. I was havin' a piss so I was."

"Of course ya were Po," teased Red.

"Yeah, we all believe ya," smirked Bishop.

"All jokin' aside now lads, it's a sore thing," said Anto.

"Ya got it Anto, that's what he had," laughed Red.

"Did ya put anythin' on it Po?" Anto continued.

"Yeah, I got some cream for it."

"Ya poor wee thing, with the poor wee sore thing," said the Bishop.

"Ya know, when ya think about it, it's worse than a sore finger ya know?" mused Red.

"How do ya figure that Red?"

"Well, ya see a sore finger is a sore thing, but a sore thing's not a sore finger?"

This got a round of laughter.

"Will yis all frig off will ya?" snarled Po.

"Well, ya had your wee self a great couple a days for sure," said Red.

"What the hell was great about them?" complained Po.

"Think about it…ya clicked with a bird…earned some money…and ended up with cream, at the strawberries."

Red was quite lucky himself. None of the potatoes Po fired at him hit their target.

End

Bird Attack

1960

Red arranged to meet Po at the top of Margaret Street at three o'clock. He glanced up at the old clock on the kitchen mantelpiece and noted the time was two forty-five. 'I'll nip down to the toilet before I go' thought Red as he pulled on his jacket. Castle Street houses had outside toilets which were twenty five yards from their back doors. Red entered the toilet and closed the door. Five minutes later he opened the door and was confronted by a very large, angry rooster. This rooster had the idea that he owned the toilet and Red was being treated as an intruder. He quickly closed the door and heard the bird's frenzied attack on the other side. This was no small bird and Red knew only too well it could do him harm. He began shouting but to no avail. He was too far from the house for anyone to hear. His mind was racing. What if no one wanted to use the toilet for the rest of the day? He could be here until tomorrow morning. He tried to stay calm and think rationally. Someone, even granny, would need the toilet before long. The sensible thing to do was just sit, be calm and wait. On the other hand the rooster might get tired or bored and go away.

It seemed like hours had passed but when he looked at his watch he noted he'd only been there thirty-five minutes. 'Time to have a look' he thought, as he quietly inched the door open. The renewed squawking and banging assured him that the rooster was not going to give up that easily.

Another ten minutes passed when Red recognised the familiar sound of his Uncle Pajoe's whistling.

"Pajoe?"

"That you Red?"

"Yeah."

"Where are ya?"

"In the toilet…that stupid rooster won't let me out."

He heard Pajoe laugh. Then the sound of his uncle shooing away the rooster.

"Ya can come out now the monster's gone."

Red opened the door slowly and looked around. A grinning Pajoe was standing there.

"Not funny, not funny a'tall, that friggin' thing's crazy."

"Well, it could give ya a doin' all right."

"At one time I thought it was gonna get through the friggin' door."

Red closed the toilet door. There were deep scratches and peck holes in the wood and that scared Red even more.

"See that?" said Red pointing to the door.

"Jasus, he was in a temper."

"That door could've been me ya know."

"True, true, bring him some seed meal next time. With roosters their belly always comes first."

"I'll remember that."

Ten minutes later Red walked into Uncle Luigi's. Po was there talking to Anto.

"There's the bastard."

"What?"

"What? Ya kept me standin' at Margaret Street corner like a spare prick at a weddin' for nearly an hour."

"Ah Jasus Po I'm sorry about that, it wasn't my fault, I swear it."

"Well, where were ya then?"

"It was a bird that kept me, ya wouldn't believe it."

"A bird?" butted in Anto. "I said it would be a bird, didn't I?"

"Yeah, yeah," mumbled Po.

"You're all flushed, ya look like she got ya in a corner and made ya sweat," continued a grinning Anto.

"Ya'll never know how close ya are Anto. I was in a corner all right and I wasn't allowed out."

"She was hot for ya then?"

"That would be understatin' it by a long way."

"Jasus H.Christ. Give us the details," pleaded Po.

"I will, I will, maybe later."

'They got the wrong type of bird' laughed Red to himself. '…but come to think about it, when ya get them angry…there's not all that much difference!'

End

The Pigeon Race

1960

Racing Pigeons were a very popular hobby in Newry and many accolades were won by the town's enthusiasts over the years. One of these was Billy Slattery, a small, sharp featured man whom Red liked. That Friday morning they met at the top of Mill Street, while Billy was on his way to pick up his daily newspaper. Red accompanied him as far as Hill Street.

"Any big races comin' up Billy?" asked Red.

"Big one tomorrow, the birds are leavin' tonight."

"How many have ya goin'?"

"Three."

"How they lookin'?"

"Good, three great birds, one in particular…fastest bird I ever had, but I can't get the bastard down."

Billy was referring to what was known as 'clocking'. The owners, or fanciers, had special 'timing clocks'. All the birds had rings attached to their legs before the race. When they arrived home, these rings were quickly removed and placed into a slot in the clock which would record the exact time and date. One problem was getting a bird to land and go into its loft so that the ring could be removed. There were stories told of birds flying around, landing on nearby trees, flying off again and landing on the loft roof. There were even times when a bird took almost fifteen minutes to go into the loft. These lost minutes could cost their owners the race and perhaps big prize money.

"Yeah, that can be a problem all right, whaddya normally do?"
"Well, as ya know the birds aren't fed before a race. So on their return home they'll be hungry. I put some seed in a tin bucket and shake it as I usually do when I'm goin' around feedin' them. They connect the sound with food and come in."
"But sometimes they take their time I suppose?"
"That's it, and in this game time is everything."
"Yeah, I can see that."
"De ya know there was a big case last year where a guy in England was in the Paris race. His bird came in early and wouldn't land. Now there was big money at stake here, thousands of pounds.
Well, he got out his shotgun and shot the bird, got the ring and clocked it. He won seven thousand in prize money. The case is still goin' on."
"Jasus."
"Right Red, I'm off this way, see ya."
"Good luck tomorrow Billy."

Red entered Uncle Luigi's where he found Po, Jumpy and Dunno eating fish and chips.
"Well boys, what's the craic?"
"Frig all," replied Po.
"How's the girlfriend Dunno?" asked Red.
"She still makin' spells?" asked Po.
"Po, now that's not right ya know. Just because a girl looks like a witch, dresses like a witch, walks like a witch and has warts doesn't mean she is a witch," said Red with a straight face.
"You two are really funny, ya know that?" snapped Dunno.
"Hi Dunno, why does she wear black all the time anyway?" asked Jumpy.

"She just likes black, so what?"

"Naw, that's not it Jumpy," butted in Po. "That's so she won't be seen at night when she's out lookin' for bat's wings and lizard's tails for her toad stew."

"Did ya ever think that if Dunno tells her what you're sayin' she might put a spell on ya ta make your wee willie fall off?" said Red seriously.

"Shit, never thought of that. Dunno, she's a lovely girl, gorgeous, I was only jokin' ya know."

"Piss off," was Dunno's reply.

Red relayed his conversation with Billy to the lads.

"That's a bitch isn't it? Imagine ya waitin' on your bird and maybe big money at stake and it's sittin' on a tree preenin' itself for twenty minutes," said Jumpy.

"Ya can understand why your man shot his bird ok," put in Dunno.

"Naw, I don't agree with that a'tall, shootin' your own bird. Not on," said Po.

"I would go along with Po on this one too," added Red.

Twenty minutes later Red and Po were walking along Hill Street when Po suddenly stopped.

"What?" asked Red.

"Shush, I'm thinkin'," said Po impatiently.

A few minutes passed.

"What for Christ's sake?" complained Red.

"Ya know, it might work, it might just friggin' work."

"What might just friggin' work?"

"The pigeons…Billy's pigeons."

Red took a deep breath.

"Po, what are ya talkin' about?"

"Look, think about this, ok? Now Billy's problem is gettin' the bird down, and ta stay down long enough ta get hold of it and get the ring off, right?"

"Right."

"So what if I could show Billy a way ta get the bird the moment it lands?"

"How would he do that?"

"Come on."

"Where?"

"Let's find Billy."

By this time Billy was home again and Po and Red found him reading his newspaper in the back garden.

"Billy."

"Well lads, what's happenin'?" asked Billy looking up.

"Billy, Red was tellin' me about your problem gettin' birds down."

"Yeah, it's a problem. Sometimes they come straight in, other times the buggers mess about for ten minutes before they land. They would drive ya' up the walls."

"Now tell me this, when ya spot them comin', what direction do they normally come from?"

"Well that depends. Usually they come in over the hill there from the east and swoop down."

Po walked away a few feet and looked around. He came back and pointed to a small tree at the bottom of the garden.

"Do they ever land in that tree?" asked Po.

"All the bloody, friggin' time. I was thinkin' about havin' it cut down."

"Is there much money on tomorrow's race Billy?"

"Yeah, there is. Prize money's big."

"Well now, suppose we could get your lead bird down fast, would there be a few bob in it?"

Billy rubbed his chin.

"If the bird is in the prize money, but only if it's in the prize money, and ya get it down fast I'll give ya a fiver each."

Po stuck out his hand.

"It's a deal."

"Now if he comes straight in the deals off. It's only if he messes about, right?"

"Right, ok, now what time de ya think your first bird will be comin' over the hill?"

Billy reached into his coat pocket and took out a bundle of notepaper. He went through it and found the piece he wanted.

"Dependin' on the weather, ya know the wind and that, somewhere around two thirty."

"Right, we'll be here about one thirty, ok?"

"Ok."

Back on the street again Red and Po turned down the hill towards home.

"Will ya tell me what you're up ta now?"

"Jasus Red it's simple. Hit me straight in the face so it did. Stickin' out like a sore thumb."

"Jasus, if ya don't tell me what you're up ta right now, there will be something else hittin' ya in the face."

"All right, all right. Now listen carefully. Now what did ya say the first thing is that attracts the birds?"

"Food."

"Right, now suppose the food was in the tree at the bottom of the garden?"

"What good would that do for frig sake? How would ya get the bugger out of the tree without him flyin' away?"

Po smiled and looked straight into Red's face.

"How do we normally do it?"

"What?"

"How do we normally do it?"

"You've lost me."

"Think Red, Pajoe, finches? The penny droppin' yet?"

Red stopped and thought for a moment.

"Ya can't be serious?"

"Why not?"

"Ya know, now that I think about it….."

"Yeah?"

"Ya mean, use the twigs with the pitch?"

"Yeah."

"Put them on the top of the tree?"

"Yeah, but will the pitch hold a pigeon?"

"Thought of that, we use thicker twigs."

"Right, ok, but how do we get the bird into the tree in the first place. It might just fly around all bloody day."

"Thought of that too. We hang a bucket of seed up in the tree, right? We tie a piece of cord to it and run it all the way back to the house. We keep pullin' the cord which will rattle the bucket."

It all began to make sense to Red now. Po's plan had begun to settle in his mind. He smiled.

"Ya know, it could work."

"It will work."

Everything was ready. Po and Red had the pitch coated twigs and the bucket of food up in the tree. They laid a ladder against the tree to help with the retrieval of the bird. Now it was all down to waiting. Red looked at his watch, it was two forty-five. He returned his gaze to the sky. Po too was scanning the hill to the east of Billy's garden. Billy was using his binoculars.

"I see one....it's him....yeah....that's him all right," Billy was pointing to the right of the hill. Red and Po saw him at the same time. He was moving fast in their direction. Po grabbed the cord and started tugging it. Billy started making a sort of clicking noise with his mouth that he normally did when calling the birds in to feed. The bird circled just once and went straight for the tree. He landed on one of Po's twigs. They all ran towards the tree. Billy climbed the ladder and retrieved the bird quite easily. He removed the ring and raced to the clock to get the timer stopped. When this was done they set about cleaning the bird and putting it back in the loft to feed.

Billy was on the phone to other local fanciers. They had a central line they could check for times. It was a bit too complicated for both Red and Po who just stood back and let Billy get on with it.

"It looks great so far...he's well in the lead...almost ten minutes I make it."

"Brilliant," said Po.

"Well, now ya have a sure-fire way to get your bird down Billy," said Red.

"Naw, we could only use this maybe one or two more times. These birds aren't stupid. They'll come in and remember the tree and give it a wide birth, but if the time stands, it'll be the best tenner I've ever spent."

The time did stand and Billy's pigeon won the race. Red and Po each got their fiver and all was well with the world…well at least the pigeon part of it.

End

Revenge 2

1960

The usual gang was gathered at Uncle Luigi's that evening when Red walked in the door. He sat with Jumpy, Kitter and Po who were already discussing the new movie showing at the Savoy.

"My favourite one with him was…what was it called Red, ya know the one we went ta see where Gregory Peck and him ended up in a big fight…?"

"Big Country?"

"That's it, what the hell was his name, I can't get it inta my head?" said Po scratching his head.

"Shit…ah…oh yeah, Charlton Heston."

"That's him, nice one Red, well he's in it too."

"What are yis talkin' about?" asked Red.

"The new movie this week, Ben Hur," answered Po.

"Yeah…heard it was brilliant."

"Well, we're all on for goin' tonight, are ya comin'?" Po asked.

"Suppose, what time?"

"Second house, starts at nine."

Red glanced at his watch…it was eight-fifteen.

"I'll go all right, but I'm not standin' in a friggin' queue."

"Well sure if we head over early it should be ok."

"Who all's goin?"

"Meself, Anto, Jumpy, Dunno and Kitter," answered Po.

They chatted for a few minutes before making their way to the Savoy. When they arrived at the cinema there was a short queue so they took their place at the end. Within fifteen minutes they were taking their seats near the back of the one and six pence section. They had paid for the one shilling seats, but no one ever checked the tickets once they were inside. Dunno and Kitter were refusing to share their crisps and sweets so a grabbing session ensued.

The lights dimmed and the advertisements, followed by the trailers of coming attractions, lit up the screen. Po elbowed Red and nodded toward Dunno who was seated next to him.

"Look what McManus has got."

Red leaned forward and looked across at Dunno, who was drinking from a bottle of John Powers Whiskey.

"Where did ya get that?" whispered Red.

"Ah ha, stole it from the auld fella. He'll think he drank it."

"Give us a sip."

Dunno passed the bottle to Red who took a mouthful.

"Frig me, don't drink it all for Christ's sake."

The theme music began for the feature film and everyone settled down to enjoy the movie. Ben Hur was an epic and over three hours long. It starred some of the leading actors of the day, like Charlton Heston, Jack Hawkins, Stephen Boyd and Hugh Griffith. After the first two exciting hours, the house lights went up for the intermission. Two girls with large trays of ice cream, crisps, minerals and sweets strapped around their necks, positioned themselves at the front of the screen and queues were already growing.

"Great isn't it?" Po said to Red.

"Plenty of action for sure."

"I'm really looking forward ta the second half...hi, look at your man," he nodded toward Dunno who was open mouthed and fast asleep. Kitter and Anto were competing to see who could lob the most peanuts into his open mouth.

"What a dick," giggled Po.

"That he is. He'll have missed the whole friggin' movie."

The lights dimmed again and the second half of the movie began. Over an hour later Red nudged Po.

"How long ta go do ya think?"

Po looked at his watch.

"About ten minutes, why?"

"Where's your ice cream carton? I have a brainwave."

"Ice cream carton, what the frig de ya want that for?"

"Where is it?" Red asked impatiently.

"Keep your knickers on, I'll look for it."

He scrimmaged around on the floor near his feet and finally found the empty carton.

"Here."

"Ta, be back in a mo."

Red stood and walked up the isle toward the toilets. When he returned he asked Po to swap seats with him.

"What are ya at Morgan?"

"It mightn't work, but it's worth a try."

"What is?"

"I filled the carton with lukewarm water."

"So?"

"Wait a minute."

Red gently took the unconscious Dunno's hand and placed his fingers in the water. He then turned back to Po.

"I heard the other day that this is how ya get sleepin' people ta pee. If it works…"

"Jasus," laughed Po, "I hope it does."

Red kept Dunno's fingers in the water for almost ten minutes to ensure success. Ben Hur ended and the lights went up in the Savoy. Both Red and Po leaned forward to check Dunno. To their delight there was a great dark stain covering the front of Dunno's trousers. Red pointed this out to the other boys while Po explained Red's experiment.

Dunno was finally awakened with much face slapping, shaking and verbal encouragement. It wasn't until they got outside the cinema that Dunno noticed his trousers.

"Jasus, I'm soakin'…what happened ta me?"

"Ya pissed your wee self Dunno."

"Frig off."

"Ya did for sure…Jasus, I can smell ya from here," said Anto.

The realisation of this fact was beginning to dawn on Dunno who, even with drink in him, was suffering the effects of acute embarrassment.

"Jasus no, this didn't happen, no, shit, ah Christ."

Sympathy was not forthcoming from any of Dunno's friends who were enjoying this moment as much as they enjoyed the movie. Eventually Dunno made a decision. There was only one course of action to be taken under these circumstances…run for it. This he did to applause and cheering from his less than sympathetic friends.

"That was a class idea," said a laughing Anto to Red on their way along Hill Street.

Red stopped and looked straight into Anto's face.

"Ya remember the night ya all got me in the graveyard?"

"Yeah."

"Well, I got Jumpy in Newcastle, remember? I got Dunno tonight. Two down….." he smiled at Anto.

"Just a minute, sure I just went along to see what was happenin' I had nothin' ta do with it."

Red didn't answer, he just walked on smiling to himself.

'Two down' he thought. 'Three more to go. I'm enjoyin' this. It's true ya know, revenge is sweet.'

End

The Great Cycle Marathon
1960

The boys gathered around a table in Uncle Luigi's Café to iron out the final plans for the next day's great cycle marathon. There were six of them going on a great adventure which would take them to Omeath, Carlingford, Greenore, Giles Quay, Dundalk, Ravensdale Forest and home. They worked out the total distance to be around forty miles.

"Right," said Anto.

"Now this is the final check list, everybody ready?"

They all had their pens and paper in front of them.

"Drinks…tick them off on your own lists as I go through them, ok?"

"Sandwiches, snacks, puncture repair kits, pumps, swimmin' gear and towels for Giles Quay and money…now on the money end, we will all need at least five bob each, ok?" Everyone nodded.

"Raincoats…in your case Dunno, a plastic bag."

"Frig off bastard; I have a raincoat so I have."

When the laughter died down Anto continued.

"And just in case we don't get home ta after dark, make sure all lights are workin' and if ya have a torch, bring it."

"Is that the lot?" asked Red.

"That's it, now we need to be leavin' here at nine o'clock at the latest in the mornin'. Make sure you're all here cause I'm not gonna be standin' round here all day waitin' on Jumpy Jones because he couldn't find his best pink knickers."

"Get stuffed," was Jumpy's surly reply.

Next morning at nine o'clock everyone was assembled and the great cycle marathon began. Even some brothers and sisters and one or two moms turned up to wave goodbye to their little angels.

They made their way down Hill Street, turning right onto Bridge Street, passing Dublin Bridge Railway Station; then across the Newry Canal bridge and left onto the Omeath Road where the first leg of their journey really began. It was six miles to Omeath Village and the cyclists made good time during the uneventful forty five minutes journey.

When they arrived in Omeath they turned left down the short hill to the pier. Shopkeepers were getting their footpaths and window displays ready for the influx of visitors that arrived every weekend from the North of Ireland. Some came from as far away as Belfast. The boys stopped at the Pier and parked their bicycles against the low granite wall.

"Is that the wee ferry boat?" Po asked Red pointing to a large open boat tied up at the pier.

"Yeah, I think that's it ok."

"It's like an over sized rowin' boat."

"That's all it is, a big rowin' boat with an outboard engine."

"That's Warrenpoint over there isn't it?" asked Kitter.

"That's it all right. It's only about a mile and a bit across I think," said Po.

"Ya could easily swim it."

"They used to have races across the Lough every year."

"If ya look along the coast there…see…just after the clump of trees, that's Rostrevor."

"Where's the Cloughmore Stone then?"

"About three quarter ways up the side of the mountain in that clear spot…can ya see it?"

"Yeah, I see it, looks small from here."

"I was up at it last year with Red; it's a big stone over nine feet high."

"Isn't there a story about it, a giant or somethin'?"

"Hi, Red, will ya tell the story about the Cloughmore stone ta Kitter."

"Move over Kitter, I wanna hear this too," said Blackie.

Red sat down beside them and began telling the story.

"Well, hundreds of years ago there was this giant called Finn McCool who lived up there in the Cooley Mountains for a while. He was waitin' on a house in North Street."

"Ach Red."

"Will ya let me tell the story, will ya?"

"All right, go on then."

"Well anyway, he heard a giant from Scotland was on his way here ta fight him. He also heard the other giant was twice his size, so he came up with a great idea."

"What?"

"Jasus will ya wait."

"Sorry."

"He got his tools out, includin' the new hammer he got in Andy Boyd's, and built an enormous baby's cot and put it outside his door."

"What for?" butted in Dunno.

"Will ya for Christ's sake listen, I'm gettin' ta that. Well, he got some baby clothes made up in his size by Josie Daly."

"Josie Daly? Ya said it was hundreds a years ago."

"It was."

"Well sure how could Josie Daly have made his clothes?"

"Have ya seen Josie Daly recently? She looks like she was around when Adam was a boy."

"Shit, but she couldn't be that old!"

"Remind me sometime ta tell ya the story about the secret potion she drinks every day."

"You're full a shit Red."

"I'm just tellin' it as it was, anyway, back to the story. Finn got all dressed up in the baby clothes and got into the cot and waited for the other giant to arrive. Sure enough, your man arrived and walked up the Cooley until he reached Finn's house. The sight of what he thought was Finn's baby in the cot scared the shit outta him. 'Frig me' says he, 'If that's the size of the friggin' baby, I don't wanna meet his da.' He took off, runnin' down the mountain and waded across the lough. Finn jumped out of the cot and got hold of a big stone which he threw after the Scottish giant. It bounced off his head and landed half ways up the Rostrevor Mountain…that's Cloughmore Stone."

"Is that supposed ta be true?" asked Dunno.

"Of course it's true."

"Sounds a bit far fetched ta me," added Jumpy.

"Jasus Christ lads, would I tell yis a lie?"

The three listeners all spoke up together.

"Yeah."

Red turned to Po and Anto.

"Did ya hear that, ya try ta teach them a bit a history and that's the thanks ya get."

"It's a downright shame," said Po.

"Disgraceful," added Anto.

Ten minutes later they were away again on the road towards Carlingford. The road ran along the base of the Cooley Mountains bordering Carlingford Lough. It took around an hour to reach the beautiful little medieval village. They explored the narrow streets and shops and a couple of the lads bought ice cream and postcards.

"Why are ya buyin' postcards Dunno? Sure you'll be home tonight," said Po.

"I'm gonna get one in every wee town we stop in. Got one in Omeath too. I promised me ma I would."

"Right," Po flicked his eyes skywards.

They found a nice grassy spot at the harbour and near the base of Carlingford Castle to have their lunch.

"Jumpy, what on earth are ya eatin'?" asked Anto. "This is my favourite sandwich…bread, butter, tomatoes, crisps and jam. Mom put in loads of chocolate as well."

"Jasus Christ, did ya hear that Red?"

"I did, that's what happened ta his leg, sure I told ya that before."

"What's wrong with ma leg," asked Jumpy.

"The short one," answered Red.

"Short one? I don't have a short leg, are ya crazy or what?"

"Jasus Jumpy, of course ya do, sure ya can see it when you're walkin'."

"Frig off will ya."

"Po…doesn't Jumpy walk like he has a short leg?"

"Yeah, why?"

"See?"

"I don't have a friggin' short leg," said Jumpy getting up and looking at his legs.

"Ok, walk down there," said Anto pointing toward the harbour.

Jumpy hadn't moved ten feet when he realised his lunch box was being attacked by chocolate raiders. Lunging backward, he had to fight tooth and nail to save his last two bars of Milk Tray.

After lunch the boys began the next and shortest leg of the journey. They turned into the village of Greenore in just under fifteen minutes. It was a quick stop since everyone's mind was now focused on Giles Quay. There were lots of long sandy beaches in this area and they were looking forward to having some fun there.

The journey to Giles Quay took almost an hour but when they arrived, and saw the beach, all thoughts of exhaustion disappeared. The boys stayed on the beach for almost two hours and did indeed have a great time. The tide was in and they went swimming. They dried off playing in the sand dunes. Anto berated Po for not bringing his bucket and spade. He was, not so politely, told to go away.

Anto called the lads together and informed them that it was time to be on the move. It was approaching five o'clock and they still had a long road ahead. Just over an hour later they parked the bicycles in Dundalk's Central Square. They wandered around the town for a while stopping to get some chips in a Park Street café. Dunno bought himself a penknife in an army surplus store. Red also bought a penknife which annoyed Po who didn't have enough money left to get one. They sat for a time in the town square.

"I wish we had time ta go see Oriel Park," said Dunno.

"Dundalk's football ground?" asked Red.

"Yeah, I hear it's a great place."

"I was in it a few times at matches with my Uncle Pajoe. Yeah, it's a fine ground all right."

"I wish I'd a known ya wanted ta see it Dunno," said Po.

"Why?"

"Ach sure I could have got someone ta open it up and show ya around so I could."

"Aye, right Po."

"Red, tell Dunno will ya, who's my uncle?"

"Which one?"

"Ya know Peter Oriel?"

"Oh, Pete, what about him?"

"Dunno doesn't believe he's my uncle."

"I didn't say that, ya said he could get ya into the ground."

"Dunno, think about it. The name of the ground is…..?"

"Oriel Park."

"…..and my uncle's name is?"

"What did ya say, Oriel?"

"Peter Oriel, they called the ground after him ya know."

"Wow."

"Very important guy ya know. He's the chairman of the club, plays centre forward and cuts the grass."

"Jasus, he must be important all right."

"Hi Dunno," Red butted in.

"Yeah?"

"If ya ever get hung for bein' smart, take my word for it, ya'll die innocent."

"Yeah? If ya say so."

At this time Po was on his back roaring with laughter.

Soon they were off again on the next leg of the journey which would bring them north on the main road to Newry. They travelled about five miles and turned off toward Ravensdale. Soon they reached a little car park cut into the forest.

"Are we goin' up the trail Red?" asked Anto.

"Yeah, why not, we can have a break up at the big oak."

"Sounds good ta me."

They climbed the twisting, steep path that wound its way up through the forest until it spilled them out into a bright clearing at the top. Standing just to the left of the clearing was a great oak tree. This was Red's favourite tree. He had been there many times in the past and either climbed halfway up or in his younger days, played beneath it. Red sat down on a wooden bench and looked up at the tree as he had done many times before, wondering how old it was. 'When Cromwell rode through here, that tree was standin' tall,' he thought.

"Yo Red?" said Anto.

"Yeah."

"What ya up ta?"

"Just lookin' at me old friend there."

"The oak?"

"Yeah."

"That's some tree."

"That it is, de ya know it's probably hundreds of years old."

"I would say that all right."

"Where's the rest of them?"

"They're all down messin' about at the stream."

"I hope ya put a life jacket and rope on Dunno."

"Never thought a that," laughed Anto.

Just then a breathless Po arrived.

"Jasus, that dopey bastard only fell in the stream."

"Dunno," said Red and Anto together.

"Naw, wrong dopey bastard, it was Kitter."

"Is he all right?"

"Wet, but ok."

"Friggin' ejit," mumbled Anto.

"He was showin' off, tryin' ta jump across…he slipped."

Red just shook his head.

"Ya know, come ta think of it, we're crazy in the first place ta let them guys come with us. I'm surprised we didn't have ta take one of them ta hospital or somethin' today."

Red knocked the wooden bench.

"Hi, we're not home yet, don't tempt fate."

Anto raised a finger.

"You're right," he also knocked the wood.

"There's another very worryin' thought Anto," said Po.

"What's that?"

"Dunno bought a penknife in Dundalk."

"Jasus, he's a cert to do himself damage with it," laughed Red.

"If you guys ever see Dunno playing with his knife and ya see me comin' along, will ya warn me? I don't wanna be anywhere near him."

They all laughed.

Before they got back to their bicycles, Kitter had fallen in the stream and cut his hand, Blackie had grazed and sprained his ankle and Dunno collided with a tree.

They arrived home in Newry that evening around nine o'clock, tired but upbeat. The boys enjoyed their great cycle marathon and promised they would do it again soon; well, all but Red, Anto and Po. They agreed they would not have another day out with the rest of the gang until they had completed medical school, studied psychiatry and had ample supplies of anti depressants…in other words, never!

End